Southern Shade

Tich Brewster
Shalisha Cooper

World Castle Publishing, LLC
Pensacola, Florida
Copyright © Tich Brewster & Shalisha Cooper 2018
Paperback ISBN: 9798891263628
eBook ISBN: 9781629898988
First Edition World Castle Publishing, LLC, March 26, 2018
http://www.worldcastlepublishing.com
Licensing Notes
Cover: Karen Fuller
Editor: Maxine Bringenberg

Table of Contents

Preface
Caleb

Life and death. Those two words mean very little to an immortal. With the gift of eternal life, we don't dwell on such things. Death passes us by every minute of the day, taking mortals to their eternal resting place, while it is nothing more than an afterthought for those of us gifted with immortality.

I'd never given it much thought until now. Death never had a reason to be on my radar, but as I stare into her eyes, those honey-brown eyes of a killer, I now know the fear that death brings. The universe has finally decided to show up and flip my world upside down. Now my heart is pounding, threatening to burst forth out of my chest. I beg death to leave, to run for the hills and let us be.

Will she?

Recognition shines in her eyes, and for an instant I think she might. I believe she will have mercy on me and flee without claiming the life of the innocent…of the one I love. Then the storm rages overhead and I know that she won't. She's come to collect regardless of whether it's right or wrong.

Suddenly, the very thing that I cared nothing for becomes the very thing that terrifies me.

Chapter One
Desiree

"Come on, Des."

Her constant whining, begging me to go out and join her for a night on the town, grates on my nerves like nails on a chalkboard. I keep my eyes on the patient chart I hold in front of me; it's hard for me to focus when she won't shut her mouth for more than half a second. She's insistent, and I wish she would just go away and bug some other poor soul.

Feeling her hovering over me, not willing to walk away without hearing my answer, I sigh. I can hear her intake of breath as she prepares to say something, most likely to continue her begging. Before she can utter a word, I speak. "No." It's clear and to the point.

But, of course, she can't just walk away. Nope. She just has to keep begging, like every other Friday. "Des, please come. If you hate it, I'll never ask you to join me. Never, ever again." If I had a penny for every time I'd heard those words from her lips, I'd be a millionaire.

Pulling the ink pen from my teeth, I finish logging the patient's progress and turn away from my nagging friend. A big puff of air leaves her lips, and I imagine her with her hands on her hips as she spins around to follow me. I lean over the counter that is the nurse's station and slip the chart into an empty slot on the rack.

She lets out several long slow breaths, and I know she is trying to think of a way to convince me to go out and party with her. One would think that after years of failed attempts, she would find a new buddy to pester. Turning to face her, I lean my hip on the counter. Looking her in the eyes, I tell her what I've told her every week for as long as we have worked here. "Look, Tracy, you know that I have zero desire to go clubbing with you. It's just not my thing."

With her hand on her hip, she purses those lips of hers. "Have you even gone to a club, like ever?"

This woman has known me since childhood—I don't know why she even bothers to ask. "No, and I don't have any desire to. Besides, I have a house to clean and a cat to feed." If only I had the ability to freeze time long enough to get out of there without having to endure any more pressure. Every weekend—I listened to her constant whining *every* weekend.

"The house can wait. As for the cat, feed her when you go home to change clothes." Tracy's lips thrust out in a pout, giving me the most pathetic puppy face I have ever been subjected to.

Shaking my head, I push myself off the counter and walk away. I'm a sucker for the puppy face, and she knows it. I need to leave before I lose my mind and cave in. Reminding myself that I have a date with my television tonight to catch up on this week's daytime soaps, I respond with, "Thanks, but no thanks."

The smell of disinfectants assaults my nose as I walk down the hall. A meal cart is against one wall and two mobile blood pressure machines are against the other. Constant beeping seeps out from under a door to my left.

Coming to a stop, I peek in the last room on this hall. This patient had been admitted early this morning with heart failure.

Heart failure. The poor girl is only ten years old—how can her heart be failing her? My heart aches for this innocent little girl. Why do children have to suffer from terminal illness? I just don't get it. Why couldn't this have happened to a serial killer instead of her? Life is so cruel.

She is sitting in bed, the covers up to her chin, and she's watching a cartoon on television. I knock on the door so I don't startle her. "Hey, sweetie, I just wanted to say goodnight before I left. I won't be back for a couple of days, but I'll see you then."

Avery's eyes are sad but she gives me her best smile. "Okay." Her voice is thick, most likely from a recent cry. She looks down at the bright green frog tucked securely in her hand. "Thank you for my frog. I named him Tulip." She hugs the stuffed animal to her chest, kissing it on the top of its head.

Seeing her cling to that stuffed animal makes me glad I took the time to buy it for her. "You're very welcome."

Avery's mother blinks her eyes open, having been woken up by our little chat. The woman has dark circles under her eyes, a sad testimonial of her sleeplessness and worry. I wave to her and she acknowledges me with a weak smile. Backing out of the room, I close the door and continue my journey toward the only exit on this side of the floor.

I follow the curve of the hall and continue to the elevators that are at the end of this hallway. I'm almost home free. "Des, you're twenty-four years old and you're living like a lonely sixty-five-year-old woman." Tracy had been so quiet that I assumed she had given up and left. Nope, just my luck. "Come on, it's time to live a little." When I don't respond, she sighs. "At least for tonight. Please?"

I press the elevator button, ignoring her in hopes that she'll take the hint and leave me alone. One could only hope. When the doors open Tracy follows me inside. This girl is my best friend.

She's supposed to be the one protecting me from peer pressure, not the one doing the pressuring. I blow out a breath, feeling defeated. "Okay, fine." I roll my eyes upon seeing her giddy smile. "I'll go with you tonight, but you have to promise me that I will never hear you beg me to do this, ever again."

"Done." Clapping her hands like a child, her goofy smile spreads even wider. She has finally broken my will, and the little she-devil is proud of herself. "I'll stop by in an hour, be showered and dressed to impress."

Oh jeez, it's going to be one of those *nights.* I can't help it; my eyes roll of their own accord. I cannot believe the mess I've just gotten myself into. The last time I went out with the girls was back when we were still in high school. Now that I am a full-time nurse, my daily schedule consists of working, cleaning house, caring for my cat, and in my spare time I like to kick back with my medical journals. I am far too busy to have any interest in partying.

On the other hand, she is right. I don't have a life. Not an exciting one anyway. I will probably grow old and die all alone. How pathetic is that?

The ding signals that the elevator has arrived at the ground level. As soon as the doors open a pair of shiny black cowboy boots enter. I look up, curious as to who the owner of those expensive boots is. Long legs in tight Wranglers, muscles bulging under that white T-shirt, and those hazel eyes stir butterflies in my belly. *Oh, my word, I've just met the man of my dreams.*

When our eyes meet, his mouth turns up in a lopsided grin that causes my heart to beat wildly. As if he can hear the commotion in my chest, his smile widens and his eyes twinkle with amusement. I open my mouth to say *hi* but my voice escapes me. He chuckles at my predicament and tips his cowboy hat with a wink.

10

A shove on my shoulder brings me out of my thoughts. "Come on." Tracy nudges me again and I move my feet, hating myself for acting like a love-struck idiot. Turning away from the most handsome man alive, I head toward the parking garage. Tracy is following closely behind me, her footsteps echoing loudly in the quiet.

I unlock my car door and finally look up at her. She has the goofiest grin on her face. No doubt it's from the fact that after all this time she finally got me to cave in and join her night of madness. As much as I want to change my mind, there is no backing out now. I'm locked into this stupid agreement. "So...I'll see you around eight o'clock?"

If Tracy's smile grows any wider, her face will split in two. "Yes. Be ready," she orders before spinning on her heel and heading toward her own car.

I wave as I drive past her black Jeep. Enthusiastically, she waves back and follows me out of the parking garage. Stopping to check for traffic before pulling out onto the road, I glance at my rearview mirror and can see her head bobbing to the beat of whatever song she's listening to.

As I turn onto Farrall Street a wave of panic hits me. I grip the steering wheel so tightly my knuckles turn white. "I don't have anything to wear," I say into the emptiness surrounding me. *What on earth will I wear tonight?* My closet consists of scrubs, a handful of worn-out T-shirts, and a couple of pairs of faded blue jeans.

Glancing out the window, the movie theater comes into view and the shock of how far I've driven brings a gasp out of me. Thank God for autopilot, because I don't remember driving this far. The blinking lights of the movie theater taunt me with the promise of refuge.

Biting my bottom lip, I contemplate pulling in. *If I were to see*

11

a movie, then I could easily avoid this soon-to-be disastrous night. It would be perfect, and she would never think to look for me here. A smile starts to spread on my face at the thought of escaping this hell. All I'd have to do would be shut off my phone, and she wouldn't have the ability to track my location.

My foot slowly presses on the brake and my hand prepares to signal my turn. Right before I press the lever, I speed up and continue my journey home. This isn't me. I don't avoid people, especially my friends. What I need to do is buck up and own this mess. Who knows, I may enjoy myself and remember what it's like to let loose and live a little.

Chapter Two
Caleb

Those perfect brown orbs pierce me to the very depths of my soul. *Who is this woman?* Her eyes venture from my feet up to my face, paying extra attention to my hips and abs. The way her nostrils flare when she appraises my body brings a lopsided grin to my face. Her eyes zero in on my lips and I can hear her heartbeat accelerate. I hope she likes what she sees, because I sure as hell love what I see.

The hospital scrubs she is wearing hide every curve of her body, but that doesn't stop me from assessing what lies underneath. Though her hair is tied on top of her head in a messy bun and her face is devoid of all make-up, this woman standing before me is the prettiest I've ever seen.

She opens her mouth; it looks as though she's going to say *hi,* but no words leave those beautiful lips of hers. I can't stop the chuckle that leaves my lips when I hear her thoughts about the way my Wranglers hug my hips. In response she intakes a breath, afraid of what I think of her. To ease her fears, I tip my hat and wink at her.

The redhead gives her a nudge on the shoulder. "Come on." Another nudge on the shoulder and her eyes finally leave mine as she stumbles out of the elevator. I don't want her to go, but now

13

is not the time to strike up a conversation with my little siren. She looks as though she's had a long day, and I have business to attend to. At least I know where I can find her—she's obviously employed here.

The steel doors close and I take my cell phone out of my back pocket. Opening the text app, I send a message to the doctor in charge of the critical patients. *On my way up.*

Before I can hit the button for the third floor, my cell phone beeps with an incoming message. *Heading to my office now.*

Shutting off the phone, I shove it back into my pocket. My thoughts immediately wonder to my dark-haired beauty with the chocolate brown eyes. I'm in this hospital once a month. I can't believe I've never seen her before. Of course, I usually make my appointments for late in the evening. Tonight is an exception, because I must be at the club early to go over the inventory.

When the doors open, I step into the hall. Antiseptic air hits my nostrils, and I automatically wrinkle my nose in disgust. The scent is too strong for my sensitive nostrils. Children talking and laughing can be heard from every door I pass. I can't imagine being a parent and having to watch my child suffer from a terminal illness. Which is exactly why I come here every month.

Passing the patient rooms, I turn right. Dr. Hebert's office is the second door on the left. Lifting my hand, I knock on his door. "Come in," he yells, and I push the door open. Dr. Hebert is leaning a hip on his desk, arms crossed. "Caleb."

I close the door behind me. "Dr. Hebert." Laying on his desk is a needle and blood collection tubes. This is a routine for us. Once a month I come in to donate my vampire blood, and Dr. Hebert uses it to cure the children who are most critical. Vampire blood restores the human body to its perfect state, without turning the person into an immortal being.

Rolling up my sleeve, I take a seat. Dr. Hebert ties a tourniquet

14

around my upper arm, then tears the wrapper from an alcohol wipe. Using his forefinger, he locates my vein. Wiping it clean, he positions the needle, bevel up, and slides it through the thin layer of skin and into the vein. Red liquid floods the tube, and once it's full, he switches it for a new one.

Ten tubes. That is what I donate every month. Very little blood is needed to restore the body, so ten usually lasts four weeks. Releasing the tourniquet, Dr. Hebert removes the needle and disposes of it in a red sharps container.

"Thank you, Mr. Shade. I have a patient in immediate need of this. Young Avery is dying of heart failure."

Heart failure at such a young age. *Have mercy*. At least now she can recover and live a normal life. "I'm glad I can help. You have my number. If you need me before our scheduled meeting, don't hesitate to call."

The doctor shakes my hand, thanking me again. Really, there is no need to thank me. No child should have to live with the torment these kids are living with. I'm happy to give my healing blood to these unfortunate and innocent children.

***

The thumping music is deafening, even out here in the parking lot. People are filing into the building, and I survey the crowd looking for a lonely woman desperate for company. After donating blood, I'm starving. Phil is bustling around, pouring drinks for several customers. Spying me, he mouths, *"Wine?"*

"Yes." Phil has been with us for a while. He knows I'm immortal; he also knows that today is my donation day and I'll be needing blood to regain my strength. One glass of blood will not be enough to sate my hunger. I'll need a warm body and fresh blood to curb my appetite.

I take a seat on a barstool while I wait for Phil to fill my drink. My focus is on the napkin in front of me with the Club

Infinity logo. When her long fingernails trail up my arm, I smile in triumph. I no longer need to go hunt for that lonely woman to sneak off into a dark corner with. She has found me.

Phil sets my wine glass down on the napkin. His eyes travel to the woman next to me, the one running her black nails along my arm. Before he can ask her what she will be drinking, I drag her off to the dance floor. I don't have the patience to listen to her life story while she slowly sips whatever concoction tickles her fancy.

Instead I take her to the dance floor, where we'll dance for a bit while I drink my glass of blood, then I'll drag her toward the back hallway and drink from her until I satisfy my appetite.

Chapter Three
Desiree

Freshly showered, I stand at my closet with a towel wrapped around my hair and stare at what little I have hanging on the rod, which is nothing suitable. "I have nothing to wear." Sure, there is a worn-out shirt with a little red cross on it that I got three years ago, after I donated blood. There is also a solid white T-shirt and a red sweater that I bought last year for the hospital's Christmas party.

The sweater is virtually new since I only wore it for the one event. I free it from the hanger and grab my best pair of jeans, worn thin with a small hole in the back pocket. This is not the ideal outfit for tonight, but it's the best I have. The world will just have to deal with it.

Just as I begin pulling the sweater over my head the doorbell rings. *What? Am I running behind?* I glance at the clock. Nope, I'm not behind schedule, she is thirty minutes early. "I'm coming," I yell. Smoothing the fabric down my waist, I race down the hallway to answer the door.

"Oh, my word," Tracy shrieks. "You are not wearing that." She gestures to my outfit.

I look down at myself. Okay, so I'm not dressed in a revealing dress with hooker heels, but I don't look like the bride of Frankenstein either. "What's wrong with my clothes?"

She steps over the threshold with a humph, kicking the door shut behind her. "This sweater is like something from the eighties. Where'd you get it, from your grandma?" Sticking her finger in her mouth, she fake gags.

Ouch. I can't believe that my best friend would dare insult me in my own home.

"Here." She hands me a plastic bag. "I came prepared."

I glance down at the name printed on the black plastic. Vanti. "You bought me clothes?" Vanti is a designer store in the mall. A store *way* out of my price range.

"Well, I didn't figure you'd have anything appropriate for the club, so I stopped and grabbed you a little somethin' somethin'."

Yes, Tracy is my best friend, and it makes sense that she would want to buy me a gift, but this? This is so out of my league.

Snapping her fingers in my face to gain my attention, she makes a shooing motion. "Hurry up and quit wastin' time."

Unlike Tracy, I didn't come from money, so most of my paycheck goes toward school loans. This is the first time that I've held designer clothing of my own. My only other experience with expensive clothing was what I borrowed from Tracy when we were growing up. Excitement runs through my veins, and I find myself bursting at the seams to try them on.

Running down the hall, I rush to strip out of my clothes and into the new ones. I'm in such a hurry that I don't bother closing the door behind me. I just want to slip into these fabulous items. If Tracy happens to peek inside, oh well, it's not like it would be the first time she saw me naked.

Standing in front of my mirror, I admire the way the clothes cling to my body in all the right places. I haven't looked this good in—well, ever. The purple halter top hugs my body and gives my breasts a push upward, exaggerating my cleavage. Black hip-hugger jeans with studs on the back pockets and silver heels complete the outfit.

The ponytail on my head is out of place—I need to fix that. Tapping my chin, I think of ways to fix my hair to match my new outfit. I could leave it down, or pull it into a bun on the top of my head. No. That's not quite the look I'm searching for.

Pulling up the Internet tab on my phone, I search hairstyles. I scroll through page after page of photos. Ten pages later, I spot the perfect style. I dig through my hair accessories drawer and retrieve a large hair clip. Twisting my hair, I pull it up, leaving a few strands to fall in loose curls around my face.

That's it. This is the perfect look for my outfit. When I walk into the living room, Tracy lets out a gasp. "You look gorgeous, Des."

Her praise makes me happy. "Thanks."

She makes a spinning motion with her finger so I twirl around, letting her get a glimpse of the front and back. A whistle leaves her lips and I smile. "Yep, you're smokin', babe."

***

By the time we arrive, the club is in full swing. Music is booming as we make our way toward the building, and the volume increases as we near the entrance. The moment I step over the threshold, vibrations from the music pulsate through the soles of my feet and up into my chest.

I have never seen a building this packed out before. Taking a moment to scan the dance floor, I'm surprised to find myself excited. Bodies are everywhere, grinding and swaying to the beat of the music. A smile quickly spreads on my face. I hadn't expected this, but the music pulsing through my body, mixing with this atmosphere, reminds me of my high school days. A thrill runs through me.

I'm reminded of what it's like to live in the moment, what

it's like to love life. Why had I been so quick to shoot her down every weekend for the last few years? Warm fingers grip my arm, giving a gentle tug. I look over my shoulder at Tracy. She has the giddiest expression on her face, and I can only assume it matches my own. Interlocking her fingers with mine, she pulls me out onto the dance floor.

We weave our way through the crowd until we find a spot with enough space for the two of us. A few whistles and catcalls come our way, but we ignore them. For now, we are just enjoying the music.

Lost in the beat, I forget about my bills, work, and responsibilities. The only thing on my mind is the lyrics to "Crazy in Love." This song is one of my favorites. Swiveling my hips, I spin around, and that's when my eyes meet his. *Oh, my word, it's him.* That sexy beast from the elevator is here in the club.

My breath hitches at the sight of him in those snug jeans, moving his body in such a provocative way. His moves are smooth and calculated. Watching him move his body like that raises my body temperature. I bite my lip to keep from mewling.

Movement catches my eye, and that's when I notice her. He's with someone…or at least he's dancing with someone. Like ice water has been tossed on me, my temperature declines at such force a shiver runs through me. Disappointed, my smile falters.

A smile lifts the corners of his mouth and the lights sparkle in his eyes. Oh, how I wish to be the woman in his arms right now. This man is what all women envision when dreaming of the perfect man. He lifts his wine glass, taking a sip of the red drink. *Wait, what?* He's dancing to this sexy music and drinking wine? Pure talent. If it were me, I'd already be wearing that delicious red right down the front of this beautiful new top.

Everything about him draws me in—his smile, his black hair and tan skin, his faded blue Wranglers that hug his backside like

20

a lover, even his dance moves. I hope that the woman in his arms is not his girlfriend; or worse, his wife.

The butterflies in my belly are dancing at the speed of light, and my heart is hammering in my chest. Again, I bite my lower lip. His eyes have been on me since the moment I spotted him, but when my teeth grip at my lip his eyes widen. One side of his mouth turns up and he winks at me.

I can feel a blush rising from my neck and spreading into my cheeks. No man has ever made me feel this way. His smile widens at the heat in my face. The moment is over all too soon when the woman in his arms gyrates against him and his attention falls back to her.

Sadness. That's what I'm feeling right now, total and utter sadness. His attention is what I crave. I want to be the one in his arms, gyrating against him, and not swaying to this music by myself.

I spin around to tell Tracy about Mr. Sexy, but she is nowhere in sight. Standing on tiptoe, I finally see her a couple of feet away dancing with a man in an old worn-out cowboy hat. At least one of us scored a dancing partner.

The song is fading and I find myself swaying to a much slower tune. It doesn't bother me that I'm standing here moving to the music by myself. There is no other man, besides my sexy Wrangler-wearing cowboy, I want to dance with. Closing my eyes, I move my body in sync with the music, imagining his arms around me. In my mind's eye, our bodies move as one and he leans in to kiss my neck.

A moment passes before I feel strong hands gripping my hips from behind, pressing my body flush against his. I don't need to open my eyes to see who it is. Everything in me recognizes him. Electricity ignites between us, warming my skin where his body is touching mine. His hands slowly travel up to my waist, his fingers splaying along my stomach.

"I haven't seen you in here before."

When those words leave his mouth, I wonder how often he comes here.

"No, you haven't."

His head leans on the crook of my neck and his breath is warm on my ear. "What's your name, darlin'?"

That southern accent makes me weak in the knees. I glance over my shoulder and into his hazel eyes. Oh, those eyes are so beautiful. "My name is Desiree. Desiree Gibson." Nerves make my voice shaky and I hope he doesn't notice.

By now, our hips are doing this seductive sway, dip, sway motion, and his fingers trace circles on my bare stomach. "A beautiful name for a beautiful lady."

Gripping my hips, he turns me in his arms. His eyes shine in the lighting, and he places his hand at the small of my back. The wine glass he had earlier is now nowhere in sight, and I'm left wondering how he had time to return it before joining me.

Just thinking of that wine glass, I imagine him sipping wine and me licking the moisture from his lips. One corner of his mouth pulls up into a smile as if he's read my mind, which is just ridiculous. There is absolutely no way that he could know the thoughts rolling around in my head. *Right?* A chuckle escapes him, and I wonder if it's possible that he can hear my thoughts.

Not wanting to ruin my evening, I choose to ignore the nagging feeling that he can read my thoughts and just rest my head on his shoulder. Tightening my arms around his neck, I get lost in the feel of him as we continue our seductive dance.

All too soon the song ends and an upbeat tune begins to blare through the speakers. He pulls away, and already I feel cold from the loss of his touch. He places a quick kiss on my cheek. "Thanks for the dance, darlin'." His southern accent seems out of place with his Hispanic features, but it's sexy as all can be.

Licking my dry lips, I notice that his eyes follow the movement of my tongue. Internally, I pump my fist in the air at this little victory. "Anytime, handsome."

His eyes stray to a spot behind me and he nods in greeting. Curious, I turn my head. Tracy is making her way to my side. Taking my hand, he plants a kiss on my knuckles. "I'll see ya around sometime?"

He wants to see me again? *Yes, you will most certainly see me again.* "Definitely."

"Good." He stays just a little longer than necessary, gazing into my eyes, then he departs with a glance over his shoulder.

"Who is Mr. McHottie?" Tracy asks.

I'm so busy watching his hips move that I'm not hearing a word she's saying. Pain radiates through my arm where she hits me. "Ow, what was that for?" Then the she-devil moves in front of me, blocking my view of him.

"Are you even paying attention to me, or are you too busy checking out Mr. McHottie back there?" She jams her thumb behind her, referencing my dance partner.

I stand on tiptoes to see where he disappeared to. Hopefully it's not in the arms of that other woman. Nope. He is now standing on the other side of the bar. Odd, does he work here? Giving Tracy my full attention, I ask, "Uh…what was the question?"

She rolls her eyes, which annoys me. "Mr. McHottie." Turning around, she searches the sea of people until she spots him behind the bar, where he is pouring a glass of wine and staring intently at us—at me. "Does he have a name?"

"Of course, he does." As the words leave my mouth I realize that I hadn't gotten his name. I had been quick to give him mine, but had failed to even ask for his. *Way to go, Desiree.*

"Well?" Tracy raises an eyebrow, showing her annoyance

23

with me.

"Well, what?" Why must this woman play twenty questions while I'm clearly trying to admire my handsome dance partner? He leans forward, resting his forearms on the top of the counter. A smile lights up his face, and his eyes haven't strayed from me this entire time.

"What is his name?" Tracy's words are slow, and she's waving her hand in front of my face.

Take a hint woman, and leave me alone to gawk at this gorgeous man.

"Oh, for crying out loud." She takes my face in her hands, forcing me to look at only her. "What is his name?"

"Huh?" Half of what she says registers, but I haven't been able to focus on her while gazing at him. It takes me a minute to remember what she had asked. "Oh." I frown. "I never asked."

"What?" Tracy shakes her head. "I can't believe we're friends. How do you dance with someone as hot as that," she nods toward him, "and not ask for his name?"

"Well, excuse me for not being up to date on this clubbing stuff." Jeez, my friend is annoying. "I just didn't think to ask."

"Well, silly, march on over there and get it…and his number." Letting go of my arms, she points in his direction, but now he's gone. Tracy's arm falls when she notices this. "Well, where did he go?"

Great. I had him in my sights and now he has disappeared. Thanks, Tracy. I scan the room. It's difficult to see with all the bodies dancing and grinding. Then there's the dim lights that add to my difficulty.

"I don't see him anywhere." Standing on my tiptoes, again, I search. My shoulders sag when I realize that he is no longer in this room. He has quite possibly left the building. "This was a bad idea. I knew I should have stayed home. Now I'll be disappointed all week."

Shaking her head, Tracy says, "No, this was a fantastic idea."

I roll my eyes. Yes, fantastic. I find the guy of my dreams, and let him disappear without getting his name and number.

She grips my shoulders, turning me back toward her. "Look, he was just behind that counter, so he obviously works here." Tapping my chin, she smiles.

It takes me a minute to understand what she's implying. Then my eyes widen in realization. Why hadn't I thought of that? Eyeing the bar, I spy two men working quickly to mix drinks for their waiting customers. My dance partner is still nowhere to be seen.

I let out a nervous breath and head toward the bar to gather the much-needed information.

Chapter Four
Caleb

I sit down in my comfy desk chair, sipping cold blood. Yes, I put my blood in wine glasses so I can drink in front of the masses. The humans occupying this joint are completely oblivious to the supernatural surrounding them. Reclining in my chair, I rest my feet on the desktop and reminisce.

When her chocolate brown eyes met mine from across the dance floor, I had been instantly captivated, just like earlier in the elevator. She was sweet perfection, with her raven black hair pulled up loosely with a few natural curls framing her beautiful face, and that top she wore showing just enough cleavage to catch my eye without revealing what lay beneath.

The way she swayed her hips to the music called to my body like a siren's song. It was like she was one with the music, and it was sexy as hell.

I noticed the way her eyes had strayed from mine momentarily to study the woman in my arms. This beauty was attracted to me. Good, because I was drawn to her as well. I couldn't wait for this song to end so I could lose the girl currently dancing with me and make my way toward my heavenly angel.

Then she had done something that completely tore me apart at the seams. She bit her lower lip as she swayed, dipping her hips low. That provocative move stole the breath from my lungs. I had just about lost all self-restraint; my fingers itched to grip her hips and press her against me as we lost ourselves to the music.

A line formed between her brows, and she appeared to be concerned about whether she held my attention. Her gaze, once again, traveled to the woman in my arms. As her eyes bore into the back of my dance partner, her nostrils flared and her heartbeat accelerated. I had to ease her worries. The woman I had chosen to dance with was nothing more than a stranger to occupy my time on the dance floor, someone I had originally planned on sneaking off with to snack from.

There was something about my angel that I was drawn to — I'd felt it when I ran into her at the hospital. The longer I stared at her beautiful face, the stronger those feelings became. In my long life, I had never felt this way about a woman.

Needing to reassure her, I waited until her eyes turned back to mine, and then I smiled. Her eyes softened and her heart sped up. Among all the other people in the crowd, her thoughts projected toward me the loudest. Opening my mind to her, I read those thoughts and couldn't stop the chuckle from leaving me. At first, she was impressed at my ability to dance with a glass of wine without spilling a drop, then her eyes and thoughts traveled the length of my body, admiring my physique.

A blush had spread into her cheeks, and it was the most beautiful thing I have ever seen. I've been around for centuries and have seen many women blush, but on her it was exquisite. The smile that curved my lips deepened, knowing that I was the cause of the heat radiating through her body.

Our dance plays over and over in my mind. The feel of her body pressed against mine, the scent of her shampoo, and the hint of a cotton candy fragrance that clung to her skin all drew me in like a sailor to a siren.

I raise my hands above my head and watch the monitors

surrounding me. There she is, standing at the bar, twirling one of her loose curls on the end of her finger. I tap my short nails on the metal arm of my desk chair. These blasted monitors don't have audio, and now I'm wishing I had purchased the ones with sound so I could hear her mystical voice.

The bartender, Phil, approaches her with a grin. I zoom in so that I can read her lips. *"Excuse me, but can you tell me the name of the man that was just back there a moment ago? He wore faded blue Wranglers and a crisp white T-shirt."*

Phil darts a glance up at the camera, knowing that I'm in my office watching the monitors. My fingernails continue tapping as I watch their interaction. He doesn't answer, but rather offers her a drink.

"She's in there asking about you."

That baritone voice startles me as I hadn't heard anyone approaching. I jerk my head to the side to look at my intruder. Alex is standing in the doorway, arms crossed. My cousin is the total opposite of me. Where I have darker skin and black hair, he is fair-skinned, with freckles and bleach blond hair.

I give him an accusing look. "Someone stole all the blood from my mini fridge. Care to explain yourself?"

Alex takes a step closer, examining my darkened eyes. "Why didn't you feed before coming in?"

Removing my feet from the desktop, I stand. "I had a snack. I had Phil pour a bag into a wine glass, and I had every intention on luring my date back to finish nourishing my body, but I was mesmerized by Desiree's captivating eyes." I glance back at the monitor for another glimpse of her.

Turning my gaze back to Alex, my nostrils flare at the smirk on my cousin's face. For whatever reason, that smirk irks my nerves and my lips pull back in a snarl. How is this funny? My body is wound tight, yearning for some oxygenated blood to

28

fuel my system, and he is standing there, completely sated and a smirk etched on his face.

A part of me wants to body slam him into the concrete floor, but I know that is just the bloodlust worming its way into my mind. I close my eyes and take a deep breath to calm the beast that is on the rise.

How long has it been since I've had a full meal? A day, two? I have done nothing but snack on a glass of blood here and a glass there. My body needs fresh, warm nutrients, or the bloodlust will take control and I'll become a wild beast full of rage and end up killing someone.

My eyes wonder back to the monitor where Desiree is sipping a drink, her eyes searching the crowd. Searching for me. I would go back out there to her, but the emotions I feel when I'm with her are strong. Mix those emotions with my hunger and I would have an uncontrollable desire to feed from her. I don't want her to see that side of me, and I'm afraid of what would happen to her if my bloodlust did overrule me.

Alex reaches in his front jeans pocket and pulls out a set of keys. Flipping through several on the massive ring, he grips a small golden key and extends his hand. "I have two bags in the mini fridge behind my desk. I'll stall her, you feed, and then get yourself out there before I decide to take her home."

"Thanks." I take the offered keys and then point a finger in his face. "You keep your grubby hands off her. She's mine."

The smirk on his face grates my nerves something fierce. "Really? Because as I see it, you still haven't given her a name, so how can you lay claim?"

I dart forward, fully intending on grabbing him by the shoulders and breaking his neck, but he has obviously read my mind. With moves as quick as lightning, Alex is standing behind me with one arm around my shoulders and the other on my head.

29

"Now, now, cousin." Alex releases his hold on me. "Don't go getting your panties in a twist."

"Panties?" I shove him. "Do I look like the panty-wearing type?" His silence and constant smirking is grating on my very last nerve. "I'll allow you to keep Desiree company until I've fed, but only because I don't want her leaving here without getting her phone number."

Chapter Five
Desiree

Slightly irritated by the lack of information, I tap my nails on the cold martini glass in my hand. This is the third song to play since my dance with Mr. McHottie, as Tracy calls him. I'm beginning to think he left the building, my presence already a distant memory of his. For the umpteenth time my eyes scan the bodies out on the dance floor. Still nothing. The man is nowhere to be found.

Where could he have gone? I thought for sure he was interested in me. *Please tell me I'm not wrong about that.* Surely the universe wouldn't be so cruel as to bring a sexy man like that into my life only to tease me with his presence.

No, I refuse to believe that I meant nothing more than a three-minute dance.

Multi-colored lights flicker on the dance floor, making it hard for my eyes to keep focus. As I continue to scan the room, my leg starts a nervous bounce. My dance partner has a name, and dang it, I intend to find out what that glorious name is so I can properly dream of my sexy man. I'll stay all night if I have to; maybe I'll even camp out front until he returns. Anything to ensure I see him again.

Ten minutes later and my shoulders slump. I've been sitting

here for what feels like an eternity and still no sexy hunk of a man. "Ugh, such is my life."

From across the room I spy Tracy having the time of her life. The new guy she's found has been stuck to her like glue. They have danced together since she sent me to find my man. How nice for her. I know I shouldn't be jealous of her, but I am. She found a guy that is totally digging her, and I find one that can't leave me quick enough. *Le sigh.*

A man sits on the barstool next to me, his hand just mere inches from my elbow. "Can I buy you a drink?"

Is the fool blind? I have a full martini in my hand, and he's asking to buy me a drink? *Weirdo.* "No." I hold up my glass as a sign that I am not in need of a drink.

Not taking the hint, he slides closer, brushing his fingers along my arm. "How about something a little warmer than that fruity mess you have there?"

Standing up, I move to a seat further down the bar and turn my attention in the opposite direction. *What a pig.* Crossing my legs, I take a sip of the apple martini. Drinking isn't really my thing, but this sweet goodness has my taste buds doing the tango. It's a party-in-my-mouth kind of drink, and I may have to order a second one before the night is over.

Warm fingers grip my arm above the elbow, and give a firm squeeze. "Now, that was rude."

Glancing down at the hand gripping me, my mouth forms a tight line. How dare that creep put his hands on me? "Get your nasty hands off me."

His nostrils flare and his eyes harden. "Come on, baby, I just want to buy you a drink."

A hand slams down on the counter between us. "I believe the lady said to take your hands off her." With one hand still on the counter, the bartender raises his other and jams a finger into the upper arm of the guy squeezing me. "I'll give you to the count of three to leave this club."

The guy hurting my arm releases a puff of air. His breath assaults my nostrils, and the stench is worse than a sewer. "This place is a buzz-kill anyway." Releasing my arm, the jerk takes off, weaving through the sea of people toward the exit.

"Thanks," I look at his nametag, "Phil."

"You're welcome." His eyes shift behind me, then he smiles and tends to other customers.

Resting my elbows on the counter, I let out a breath. Some people really know how to damper the mood. Running my finger over the rim of my glass, I dip my finger inside and lick the stickiness off. Lost in my own little world, I never hear any footsteps, but who can hear a thing with this music blaring and people shouting above the noise? When a hand clasps my shoulder it startles me. I jump and nearly spill my drink down the front of my shirt.

Hoping that it's my sexy cowboy, I smile and turn around, but my smile fades when I spy the blond-haired man standing there. He extends his hand. "Hello."

I glance at the offered hand like it will suddenly grow fangs and bite my fingers off. The hesitation causes him to push it out further, clearly unwilling to be ignored. In hopes of rushing him along, I accept his hand, giving him an awkward shake. "Hi. I'm actually waiting for someone."

Bringing my hand to his lips, he plants a gentle kiss to my knuckles. "So, what's your name?" Clearly, he is ignoring the fact that I'm waiting for someone.

Pulling back my hand, I frown when his grip tightens, holding me in place. *Ugh, does this man have no manners?* I really don't feel like dealing with another creep. "Uh." I look down at our joined hands. "Can I have my hand back? I kind of need it for work on Tuesday."

The multi-color lights twinkle in his eyes, changing the color of his irises. Glancing up to a spot above the bar, he smirks and my eyes immediately follow the trail his had followed. Hanging from the ceiling is a surveillance camera. I hadn't noticed that before. Then again, I wasn't scoping the place for high tech security either.

A tug on my hand pulls my attention from the tiny camera. Pulling me off the barstool, his eyes examine me from head to toe. Grunting in approval, a smirk settles on his face when he looks back up at the camera.

Okay, this creep has me feeling highly exposed and nervous. His manners are somewhat worse than the other guy's. At least the other guy didn't mentally rip my clothes off and grope me telepathically. I swallow, hoping to get some moisture back into my dry throat. Straightening my spine, I demand, "My hand. Now." Hopefully he doesn't notice the slight crack in my voice.

The grip on my hand loosens and he gives me a wide smile. "No need to fear me, sweetheart. I don't bite. Well, not much anyway."

What a fruitcake. "Look, I don't know who you are, but could you just leave me alone and bug someone else? Maybe find a willing girl and dance off some of that energy you have." *Get a clue, moron, I do not want you touching me. I just want my cowboy, and maybe to get a goodnight kiss while I'm at it.*

He chuckles, and I'm left wondering if I just said that out loud. Surely I hadn't. I'm fairly certain that I had my jaw clamped shut. *Oh no. Now he is laughing. Do I have something on my face? A booger on the tip of nose? Why is he laughing at me?*

"I'm sorry." His apology is sincere but it doesn't make me feel any better. "You're adorable when you're flustered."

"What?" Okay, either this man has lost his mind and gone

34

crazy, or he is a psychic and can read my mind. Damn. I really hope it's not the latter.

Chapter Six
Caleb

I'm sitting in my cozy desk chair watching my cousin act like a fool, knowing full well that I'm watching his every move. Some days I wish we weren't related—then I wouldn't have to deal with this hellhole he calls a club. Sometimes I feel like I spend more time helping him run this stupid joint than I spend on my own ranch. It's a good thing I have the money to keep ranch hands—otherwise my damn family business would crumble to the ground.

Squeezing the bag, I drain the last of the blood and toss the empty piece of plastic in the trash. The thing I hate about bagged blood is that it never satisfies that deep hunger, it just takes the edge off. What I need is a warm body with rich oxygenated blood flowing through its veins.

Running my hand over my mouth, I make sure there is no bloody residue on my face before I head back out and save Desiree from the evil clutches of my cousin. As I stand, I notice Alex touching Desiree's face. He's just brushing a lock of hair behind her ear, but it makes me so angry I'm seeing red. "Why do I have to be related to this moron?"

As soon as the question leaves my lips, Alex looks up at the camera and winks at me. What a prick. I hope he feels my pain someday. Knowing he can't see me but needing to show him how I feel, I give the monitor the bird then leave the office. Some days I wonder why I ever agreed to help finance and run his stupid club.

As I trek down the narrow hall toward the main part of the club, the music grows louder and the bass vibrates up my legs. Up ahead I can see Phil pouring a line of drinks for customers. Alex's mental appraisal of Desiree's body is projecting loud and clear to my mind, angering me further.

When I step around the corner, his eyes meet mine. He is wearing a smirk, and I'd give anything to punch him senseless. Directing his telepathic dialogue to me, he says, *Now I know why you're so attracted to her. She smells different, almost powerful.* He reaches up and pinches her chin.

Rage is boiling under my skin, but I must keep my cool. After all, I'm in a club surrounded by humans. He must see the red flecks sparkling in my eyes, because he raises his hands in surrender and takes a step back.

Desiree's shoulders relax, and it puts a smile on my face knowing that she was not enjoying Alex's touch. Rounding the bar, I step in front of her in time to halt her from leaving. Her eyes light up when she sees me, and it warms my heart. A feeling I'm not used to.

"Hey, darlin', I heard you've been lookin' for me. I'm glad to see that you're still here." I take her hand and kiss the tender spot just below her knuckles. The blush tinting her cheeks brings a smile to my face. It amazes me that in all the centuries I have walked this earth, I have never felt deeply drawn to any woman—until now. There is just something about Desiree that connects with me, spirit and soul.

Knuckles popping draws her attention away from me, and her eyes nervously shift over my shoulder, toward Alex. She takes a step closer to me, and I feel like pounding my chest like a damn ape. "Yes, I have been looking for you." She's still looking at Alex, and I can't help myself, I listen in on her thoughts. *Why on earth are you still around? You're creeping me out. Take a hint already.*

I chuckle, and that small act earns me her attention. "I see you met my cousin, Alex."

"Your cousin?" Her brows furrow and she looks completely confused. "Are one of you adopted? You look nothing alike." Pointing a finger at me, she says, "You've got Hispanic features, and he looks like a beach bum."

Oh, I love her humor. I laugh out loud, not caring that people turn to stare. She hit the nail on the head. That question has crossed my mind more than once since Alex and I were kids. "If only. But sadly, yes, I'm related to the beach-blond bum."

Alex raises a brow, clearly not amused. "I may be a beach-blond, but at least I'm not a Hispanic hick." He shakes his head. "That's just not right, dude."

A hick I am not. Do I have a southern accent? Yes, but I am not a damn hick. "Hey, I don't have that blasted hillbilly accent." And who says that a Hispanic can't be a cowboy? Not all of us wear sombreros and strum guitars, or wear bandanas and walk around acting like gangsters. Most of us are normal human beings. Has he not seen our ancestors? They wore cowboy hats and cowboy boots. I swear, that blond hair has damaged that pea-sized brain of his.

"Whatever." Alex takes Desiree by the hand and bows his head. Bows his head? Since when did he discover mannerisms? "It was nice meeting you." Not bothering to look at me, he walks off in the direction I'd just come from. "I'll be in the office if you need me."

"Office?" Desiree's eyes grow wide in shock. "He owns this joint?"

The look on her face makes me smile. "Yes, he owns half of this place."

She tilts her head back in that *ah, ha* kind of way. "Figures. He doesn't quite seem like the business type. Do you know the co-owner? I hope he's not as creepy as your cousin. No offense."

There is no holding back the laugh that erupts from me. It's loud and startles her. Using both hands, she holds her martini as if it's her best friend. I bite the inside of my cheek so I don't scare her off with more uncontrolled laughter. "Yes, I do know the co-owner, and no, he's not the douche that Alex is."

She sips her martini, and I swear she licks her lips just to taunt me. My nostrils flare; I'm doing everything within my power to keep myself restrained. Those innocent eyes of hers show that she has zero idea of the effect she has on me.

I extend my hand. "My name is Caleb Shade." Her smile brightens her whole face. "And I'm the co-owner of this establishment."

"You?"

Judging by the look on her face, she either doesn't believe me or doesn't think I'm the business type. I allow her a moment to scrutinize me. There's quite a bit about me she may have a hard time believing. Like the fact that I'm a vampire. "Yes, but I'm only here on the weekends. My day job is a little dirtier than this."

I lean my hip against the counter and watch the expressions that cross her face. It's clear to see she took my statement to mean something on the sexual side. "Dirtier?" The thoughts running through her mind apparently make her uneasy, as her voice is nothing but a whisper. Listening in on her thoughts, I see why she's timid. She's picturing me with whips and cuffs.

"By dirtier, I simply mean that I own a ranch across town." Now that I've put her mind at ease, she breathes a sigh of relief.

When I told her that my job was dirtier, she thought I meant the whole fifty shades thing. Not my style. Hopefully that look on her face means it's not her style either.

"Oh, how fun." She sets her drink down and clasps her hands together. "My grandma used to take me out to the local farm when I was little. I remember watching her milk the cows. After we got our milk, we'd gather eggs from the chickens to bring home, along with the fresh milk."

That memory obviously sparks something in her, because the look in her eye is distant. Not in a bad way, she just looks like she is lost in a good memory. It makes me want to give her something from her past, even if it's just a small piece. I'd do anything to keep that love shining in the depths of her eyes.

I take her hand. "Maybe I'll bring you out to the ranch sometime."

She bites her bottom lip, probably in an attempt to calm the excitement building within her. "I'd love that."

Good. I look forward to sharing pieces of myself with her.

Chapter Seven
Desiree

Chatting with Caleb is fascinating. He's full of all kinds of information, even useless information. Who else on earth would know the history of the land down the road from the local school? I mean, it has been empty land since my grandma was raising children.

I can hear the clog, clog, clog of Tracy's heels long before she appears at my side. The dark circles forming under her eyes is a clear indicator that her body has had all the excitement it can handle for one day. I guess that's what happens when you pull a twelve-hour shift and then decide to hit the club immediately after.

She sits with an audible humph. "This has been the best night of my life." Stretching her arms out on top of the counter, she leans forward to rest her head between them. "But I'm exhausted. I may need you to drive us home."

Only now do I glance down at my watch. It's nearly three in the morning. How did time fly by so quickly? I look around and notice that the place is empty. The music is still blaring through the speakers, but not a single customer remains. Now I feel guilty. Have I been keeping Caleb and his cousin from properly shutting down the club and heading home for a decent night's sleep?

"I'm sorry. I didn't realize what time it was." I move to stand, and Caleb stills my movements with a hand on my thigh.

His eyes are kind, and the heat from his hand warms me to the very inner depths of my soul, which is a foreign feeling to me. "Don't be sorry, darlin'. I really did enjoy your company." The way he says darlin' stirs the butterflies in my belly, and the sensation almost makes me giddy. That is something I could get used to.

Being in his presence, talking about everything and nothing, brings me such joy and peace. I don't want to go, but Tracy is already dozing off, and the last thing I need is to have her falling off that stool and cracking her skull open. "I should probably get her home."

He doesn't say anything, just nods in agreement. If only I could freeze time and stay in this happy little bubble for all eternity. The corner of his mouth lifts, and again I'm left wondering if he can somehow read my mind. He seems to smile at just the right time as the babbling in my head begins.

Alex rounds the corner with a wine glass in hand. Isn't it too late, or too early in the morning, to be drinking? Whatever floats his boat, I guess. He smirks and takes a seat next to Tracy. His eyes glisten with curiosity as he studies her limp form.

"Come on, darlin'. I'll walk you out to your car." Caleb stands and lifts Tracy as if she weighs nothing more than a feather. She mumbles something incoherent, rubs a hand over her face, then relaxes in Caleb's arms.

I bend over and pick up her purse, riffling through the contents in search of her car keys. Good grief. How much stuff could a person keep in their dang purse? This thing is a junk collector for pens, coffee pods, paperclips, and other odds and ends. And she said I was living like an old granny—has she even seen the inside of her purse?

Finally, I find the keys at the bottom corner, hidden under a travel pack of tissues. Caleb leads the way out of the club and to the only remaining vehicle in the lot, aside from the black truck and Maserati parked at the very back. As soon as the locks pop up he situates Tracy in the back seat.

I really hope to see him again. It's been far too long since I have felt like this. No, that's not quite right. I have never felt this alive before. He has awakened parts of me that I didn't even know were slumbering.

Caleb shuts the car door and moves to my side. His eyes travel to my cleavage briefly before he takes my hand and rubs his thumb along my knuckles. The touch is soft and brings a smile to my face. "How about dinner tomorrow night?"

"Okay." *Okay?* That's all my brain could come up with? I mentally give myself the facepalm. I can't believe I said something so stupid when I should have responded with *yes*, or *I'd love to*.

Amusement lights his features. "Good." He holds out his hand. "Give me your phone and I'll program my number." I all to eagerly hand him my cell phone. His fingers move quickly on the screen. "Done. And I sent a text to my phone so I can get you programmed in mine as well."

Joy rises in me. He wants to program my number into his phone? I have no idea why my inner voice is acting like a high school girl, but his interest in me excites me on a whole new level. "Awesome. I look forward to tomorrow."

The expression on his face mirrors what I'm feeling. "Me too."

Reluctantly, I open the car door and crawl in behind the wheel. I would much rather stay here with Caleb, but I have Tracy to tend to. He stuffs his hands in his front pockets, hooking his thumbs in the belt loops.

Oh, my word, that is sexy as hell.

43

I wave, then put the car in drive and start toward the street. In the rearview mirror, I see him. He stands in the same spot, watching me until I'm no longer in sight.

Chapter Eight
Caleb

The moment I step foot back inside the club, Alex gives me a quizzical look. "You know, there's something different about her, something old and powerful."

I know he's right. The instant my hands touched her skin I felt a magnificent power radiating off her, one different from any I have ever felt. Desiree is definitely human—there is zero trace of any vampirism flowing through her. Though, whatever lies within her is just as powerful. "I know. I felt it."

Alex wipes his glass clean then puts it in its rightful place. He tilts his head, as he always does when he is trying to solve a puzzle. "I've never encountered anyone quite like her." Shrugging his shoulders, he continues his task of wiping the counter clean. "Well, I hope you got her number, because her friend was smokin' hot."

I roll my eyes at my cousin's unfiltered tongue. Alex is what some might consider a man whore. Where others might comment on Desiree's friend as pretty or beautiful, my cousin goes straight to the hot factor. "There ain't a gentlemanly bone in your body, is there?"

His shoulders shake with his laughter. "Gentlemanly? We're not in the 1800s, cousin. This is 2017. In case you haven't noticed, proper mannerisms went out the door years ago."

I pick up a lone napkin, wad it up, and throw it at his head. "Thanks, Einstein." It still baffles me that we come from the same bloodline. Polar opposites, that is what we are, what we have always been. After all these years, I still wonder if my aunt was given the wrong baby at birth.

Shaking my head, I leave him to his cleaning and trek to my office. I'm ready to pack up my belongings and head home, but first I want to send a quick text to Desiree to make sure she made it home okay, and to confirm a time for our date tomorrow. *Just checking to see that you made it home safe.*

Her response is instantaneous. *Yes, I did. Thank you for checking up on me.*

Wow, she must have had her phone in hand because that was quick. I shoot off another text. *How does 7pm sound? I can swing by and pick you up.*

Sounds perfect. I can't wait. Again, her response is immediate. I picture her sitting on her bed, phone in hand, like she is anticipating my texts. That image makes me feel on top of the world, imagining my brown-eyed beauty anxious for my words.

My fingers fly across the screen. *Where do you live, darlin'?*

I shut down the monitors on my desk as I await her reply, which takes all of ten seconds to appear. *On the north corner of 7th and Bell Ave.*

I'll see you tomorrow evenin'. Have sweet dreams, darlin'.

I wait a couple of minutes in case she sends a reply, but it doesn't come. Stuffing my cell phone back into my pocket, I organize my desk. There is nothing that drives me crazier than a messy workspace.

Once everything is in its rightful place, I slide the chair forward and turn off the lamp. I turn to leave, but my mini fridge catches my eye. There is no doubt in my mind that I had a full

46

stock of blood bags in there just the other day. If Alex wasn't the thief, who was?

Only the two of us have a key to this office. Though I have checked, double checked, and even triple checked this evening, I reach down and pull the door open. Still empty. This doesn't sit well with me. Truth be told, if the thief had asked to retrieve a bag or two, I would have happily agreed. Heck, if he or she would have left a note, I would have shrugged my shoulders and brushed it off. But theft is going too far.

Slamming the little metal door, I make a mental note to call the blood bank and have a shipment sent over. While I'm at it, maybe I should invest in a chain and lock for that blasted fridge. Nothing angers me more than a thief.

Pushing my emotions aside, I lock up my office. When I walk around the corner, Alex is out on the dance floor. Music is still blaring out of the speakers, and my cousin is flexing his hips in a hideous dance move that reminds me of something from the sixties.

I shout a goodbye to Alex on my way to the door. Either he doesn't hear me over the music or he's ignoring me. Shrugging my shoulders, I push open the door. The automatic lock clicks into place the moment the door closes behind me.

The streets are devoid of traffic, as they should be at this hour. Humming from the tall street lights in the parking lot echoes around me. My truck is parked around the back, and as I walk that direction the night air chills dramatically. The sudden shift in the air raises the hairs on my arms.

Stopping in my tracks, I glance around. Nothing is out of place, and I don't sense another supernatural being. Nonetheless, I can't get past the nagging dread that something evil is about to take place.

Chapter Nine
Desiree

The morning sun pierces through my eyelids like a beacon, waking me from the best dream of my life, where a sexy, dark-skinned cowboy presses my body flush against his as we sway to the beat of the music.

It's far too early for this nonsense. Doesn't Mother Nature know that I need my beauty sleep? I roll over and groan. Normally I'm a morning person, but today I'm exhausted. Stretching my legs, I sit up with a start when my foot touches warm skin. When I see Tracy's red hair peeking out from the blanket, I remember the events of last night.

Instead of taking her home last night, I'd brought her here and tucked her into my bed.

Now that I'm awake, I slip out of bed and gather my clothes for a shower. Thoughts of Caleb fill my mind. That man is every woman's dream come true, and I can't believe he asked me out for a date. The smile forming on my face is so wide my cheeks begin to hurt.

Quietly slipping out of the door, I start down the hall, but then hear my phone ding with an incoming text. Rushing back inside, I grab it off the nightstand so it doesn't wake Tracy. The last thing I need is for her to wake before she's had enough sleep.

Moody would not even begin to describe her if that were to happen—she would be more like the wicked witch of the west.

Swiping my finger across the screen, I see it's a text from Caleb. I open the message. *Mornin', darlin'.* His southern drawl is adorable.

Immediately following is another message, a picture message. A dusty cowboy hat is shading his face from the sun, and a few specks of dirt dot his face. It's plain to see that he has been working outside, and now I'm wondering what kind of ranch work he's been doing. His luscious lips are curved upward, lighting his eyes.

Joy fills my heart and I hug my phone to my chest. How is it that this man can awaken my body and soul after knowing him for only a few hours? If I believed in soul mates I would claim he was mine, but I don't believe in such things. That stuff is for fairytales. Yet he makes me feel whole and complete.

My phone dings again and I pull it back to view the screen. His next message says, *Duty calls, I'll see ya tonight.*

The fabric of the blanket rustles as Tracy rolls over. Silently cursing myself, I flip the button on the side of my phone to switch the ringer to vibrate. Heavy snores rumble from her, and I know, if left alone, she will most likely sleep until noon. Last night she had quite a bit to drink, that plus the fact we were out until three in the morning after working a twelve-hour shift at the hospital, so her body needs the rest.

I know I'll probably regret getting up this early—it's just after seven in the morning. Hopefully I'll find time later to take a catnap so I don't doze off this evening when I'm with Caleb. How embarrassing would that be?

While I wait for the water to get warm I open the music app on my phone and hit play. This music list is a nice mixture of country, with a little hip hop and rock and roll thrown in. Most

people hate when I turn on my playlist because of the variety —
some hate one style or the other.

"Southern Gentleman" is the first song to play, and it reminds
me of Caleb. Everything about him is gentlemanly, from the way
he talks to his attitude toward others. I have never been a big fan
on southern twang, but on him it makes my heart melt.

I sway to the music. Luke Bryan is my favorite country artist,
and to be honest, his music takes up most of my playlist. As my
hips sway, I imagine Caleb behind me with his arms around my
waist, our bodies moving as one.

Steam rises above the shower curtain, signaling for me to get
in. With a sigh, I stop my dancing and strip for my shower. I sing
as I wash my hair, my hips moving to the beat of the music. It
doesn't take me long to wash — two songs later and I'm stepping
out of the tub.

Freshly showered and feeling refreshed, I pad down the
hallway to the kitchen. Now that I'm fully awake, my stomach
is growling loud enough to wake the dead. I really should have
gone shopping yesterday. My refrigerator is bare except for the
package of cheese in the drawer. The cupboards aren't much
better. I have a loaf of bread and a box of cereal.

The cereal sounds good, but alas, I have no milk. Toast it is.
I toss two slices of bread in the toaster and brew a cup of coffee.
Inserting the last K-Cup into the coffeemaker, I jot down a note
to pick up another box. There is no way I'll survive tomorrow
without a cup of my precious java.

While I'm waiting on the toaster and Keurig, I pick up my
phone and stare at the picture Caleb sent me this morning. His
brilliant hazel eyes sparkling in the light of the sun. I trace the line
of his jaw. This man is what dreams are made of. He is absolutely
perfect.

The toast pops up and the Keurig spits the last of the brew

into my cup. I take the butter out of the fridge and slather some on my toast, then remove my cup from the base of the coffeemaker. Sitting at the table, I quickly save his picture on my phone and set it as his contact image before devouring my breakfast.

***

Tracy is still sleeping soundly, so I leave her tucked in bed and head out to get a few groceries. Lord knows that woman will be starving when she wakes up.

The grocery store is packed today, and I'm finding it difficult to maneuver through the aisles. A woman with four small children passes by, and the youngest giggles and waves at me from his seat inside the shopping cart. I love children. Someday when my life settles down and I find Mr. Right, I plan to have two or three.

Speaking of Mr. Right, my mind travels back to last night — to Caleb. I can't help but wonder if there is a chance that he could be my Mr. Right. Only time will tell, I guess. For now, I'm going to sit back and see where life's journey takes us.

I squeeze between two women and grab a couple of cucumbers. Obviously, I picked the wrong day to go shopping — it's a madhouse in here. A shopping cart hits the back of my foot and I nearly topple over. The man pushing said cart never even bothers to look my way and apologize. What a rude and selfish world we live in.

After a couple of other rude customers, I've had enough. I push my cart toward the front of the store. I have what I came for anyway — milk, eggs, bacon, fruit, veggies, and most importantly, coffee.

Chapter Ten
Caleb

This morning when I pay a visit to the horses, they greet me with excitement. Of course, that could be because a sack of apples dangles from my fingers. Billy had beat me to the stables and had groomed them before tending to the other animals.

Badger's lips move in anticipation of his treat. "Hey there, Badger." The moment my hand moves toward him, he bends his head to retrieve his fruit. I run my hand along his head as he chews.

Normally I spend Saturday mornings with Badger, giving him the exercise and companionship we both crave. Today, however, I'm in a rush to get the daily chores done so I can start preparing for my day with Desiree.

Giving Badger one last stroke, I leave the stable and head for the barn. Billy and Joe are milking the cows, neither looking my way when I enter. "How's it goin' in here?" I ask.

Billy's eyes never stray from his task at hand. "Great." He releases the udders and scoots his stool away. "Just finished."

Joe stands. "Yep, me too." Using the sleeve of his shirt, he wipes the sweat from his forehead. "David is taking care of the garden and Mike is gathering eggs."

"Done." Mike sets a basket of eggs down just inside the barn.

"Today's chores are done. Well, except for feeding the pigs."

I point at my muddy boots. "Took care of 'em already." This is such a nice start to my day. I pick up the bucket of milk next to Billy then reach for the one at Joe's feet, and carry them to the other side of the barn, hefting them onto the counter for the guys to bottle.

I don't have a lot of time on my hands today—I still need to head over to the club and check the books and do inventory. This is what I had planned on doing last night, but a certain dark-haired beauty held me captive. Not that I'm complaining—I don't regret a minute I spent with her. But the truth is, Alex isn't the best at handling the financial part of the business. He'd rather be out there with his customers flirting and doing only God knows what.

I gather a few of the eggs from the basket at my feet and carry them with me so I can wash and refrigerate them. One of the biggest misconceptions is that vampires don't eat, when in fact we eat just like everybody else. True, we don't need the nutrients to survive, but the food is satisfying to the stomach nonetheless.

The trek back to the house is quiet. All the noise from the animals is a good distance behind me, and the noise from the workhouse where we process the goods is at an equal distance in the opposite direction.

I take the time to stop and pick a few roses along the way. They're beautiful and fragrant, just like Desiree. I think I may have found *the one* to spend eternity with. Her spirit is full of love and hope, and I wish to give her all that her heart desires. Strange, I know, considering I just met the girl.

My phone chimes and I check it. It's a text from Desiree. *Do I need fancy or casual attire?*

I can't help but chuckle. I guess I should have told her last night whether she would need fancy clothing. Once she gets to know me, she'll understand that I'm all about my Wranglers and boots. There ain't a fancy bone in my body.

I type a reply. *Casual, darlin'.*

Her response is a smiley face. I haven't gotten into the whole emoji texting thing. To me, smiley faces are for those in their adolescence, not for grown men. Alex, on the other hand, texts emojis with every damn text he sends. Her next text has words, thank the Lord. *Good, I'm a nurse. My closet consists of scrubs and not much else.*

My thoughts travel back to our run-in at the hospital. The moment her chocolate-brown eyes met mine, I was a lost cause. Her soul called to mine, beckoning me with a flick of its wispy little finger, and I was helpless to stop myself from following.

Ding. I glance down at my phone.

Again, she sends an emoji. A laughing face with tears shooting from its eyes. I suppose this is something I'll have to get used to. With Alex, I ignore those damn faces and delete them from my phone. I refuse to do that with Desiree. Every emoji she sends will stay on my phone, only because it's from her.

Cringing, I open the emoji tab on my text and send her a smiley face. Stuffing the phone back in my pocket, I shake my head. I can't believe I just sent a damn smiley face over the phone. Hell has officially frozen over.

This girl has definitely gotten under my skin. If it had been anyone else, and I mean anyone else, I would not have responded at all to that damn emoji crap.

Chapter Eleven
Desiree

I glance down at my phone. He sent me a smiley face emoji. A giggle erupts from me, because I don't see Caleb as the emoji kind of guy. Maybe it's because he's attracted to me...or I guess he could just be one of those guys that uses those texting faces. I don't know. What I do know is that we have a date tonight, and I need to go shopping for something to wear. The last thing I want to do is show up wearing the same outfit I wore last night; talk about a disaster.

Unlocking the front door, I head to the kitchen to put away the groceries. The house is silent except for the tick-tock of the clock. I'm guessing that means Tracy is still curled up in my bed, sound asleep.

If only I could be as lucky. Sleep is something I desperately need, but I'm not willing to waste time when I have a date to get ready for. With my luck, if I did lay down for a nap, I'd end up sleeping through our date. As soon as I'm done putting this food away I'm waking her up. I need clothes for tonight and I have absolutely no idea what to buy. Tracy, on the other hand, is a fashionista—she'll be able to help me with my dilemma.

It doesn't take me long to get the groceries put away. Tossing the plastic bags in the trash, I head down the hall. Tracy is right where I left her, snuggled up in my comforter, still sawing logs. In this position she reminds me of a child, curled up on her side with her knees drawn in. I shake her leg and she moans in protest.

"Tracy." I give her leg another firm shake and she rolls away from me, throwing the comforter over her head like a rebellious teenager. "Hey, I need you to get up so we can go shopping for clothes."

At the mention of clothes shopping, she shoots out of bed. Untangling the blanket from her legs, she tosses it back onto the bed before eyeing me with a grin. "Did you just say shopping? For clothes?" I nod and a huge grin breaks out on her face. "Sweet. The gods have heard my cry."

Oh, my goodness, she is dramatic as all can be. I roll my eyes at her and leave her to find her shoes and brush her hair. It doesn't take her long, and within minutes she's in the living room with her purse in hand.

We head out the door and to her car. I don't remember the last time I went shopping for anything other than groceries. Even my scrubs I purchase online. I've been a workaholic since graduating nursing school, and a homebody on my days off. This is a refreshing change.

The mall isn't far, just a six-minute car ride. I have no idea where to even look or which stores to visit, so I just fall in line behind Tracy. She frequents this place, so I'm confident she will know where to shop.

Immediately she heads up the escalator. For a Saturday afternoon, the mall isn't as packed as I thought it would be. Which is nice, because I'm not really a social person. I'm an introvert and love my space.

Tracy turns around, hands on hips, and taps her foot in impatience. "Hurry up, Des. You're so dang slow."

I frown at her. *Slow?* That's an exaggeration. Just because I don't climb up the stairs of a moving escalator does not mean that I'm slow. It just means I like to enjoy myself on my day off, and not try to get in a cardio workout on a moving staircase. There is a reason this thing moves from one floor to the next, so you don't have to climb.

"Hey, I am not slow. I just don't enjoy doing cardio exercise on my day off." I stomp up the last couple of steps and follow her around the corner.

The Vanti sign is just up ahead, and I know this is where she's leading me. I love the designer clothes they carry, but I also don't have that kind of cash at my disposal. My financial situation isn't unknown to her, so I'm curious why she would bring me here. Biting my lip, I contemplate telling her this store is a no go.

Tracy spins on her heel, looking directly into my eyes. "Look, I know that your bank account isn't all it could be. I know that you spend a lot of your hard-earned money helping to support your grandma." I nod, but am unsure where she is going with this. "That being said, I am funding this shopping spree."

I shake my head. There is no way I can allow her to do such a thing. Besides, she bought my outfit for last night. If she buys my outfit for tonight, it'd be too much.

"You may as well forget trying to talk me out of this." She reaches out and takes my hand. "I have the money, and this is what I want to do with it."

Tears are filling my eyes and her face becomes blurry. I don't know what to say. Tracy is my best friend, my confidant. This act of kindness, even from her, is stirring so many emotions within me, and I can't contain them. I let the tears fall and she wipes them away with her thumbs.

"Don't get all weepy on me or I'll start crying, and you know I hate to cry." She straightens her spine. "Come on, let's find you an outfit." Just as she's about to start toward Vanti, she furrows her brows and cocks her head. "I don't remember much about last night. Who are you dating?"

Yeah, she was pretty smashed. A smile quickly spreads from ear-to-ear. "His name is Caleb."

She purses her lips as she thinks. I can tell when it finally registers, because her eyes light up. "Ooh, is he that super-hot Latin cowboy?" I nod, and she lifts her hand for a high-five. "Good job, Des, Mr. McHottie is smokin'."

"Oh, jeez." I shake my head at her crazy nickname for him. "Mr. McHottie has a name, and it's Caleb."

"Yeah, yeah." Tracy grabs my hand and drags me toward the store. "Let's get you an outfit that will make him want a second date."

I really hope that doesn't translate into a trashy outfit. The last thing I want is for Caleb to think I'm some nympho itching to add him to my conquest list.

Chapter Twelve
Caleb

After cleaning up around the house, I go out to the stable to see Badger. Deep in my bones there is an itch that needs scratching, so I saddle him up and take him for a ride. Out of all the horses on this ranch, Badger is my favorite. He's the one I go to when I need to talk or when I just need quiet companionship. Of course, I know a horse can't carry on a conversation, but dang if he doesn't offer comfort and understanding when I need it.

I ride him out toward the end of my property and slide off his back. Reaching in my pocket, I pull out an apple and cut a piece off for him. "Badger, you're my best boy." He blows air through his lips, making a raspberry noise, in response.

Feeding him another piece of apple, I tell him about Desiree. He listens, making happy noises when I talk of her beauty and kindness. It's ridiculous to think he understands a word coming out of my mouth, but I take his nods and raspberry noises as confirmation that he thinks Desiree is a good companion for me.

When I look down at my watch, I realize that we've been out here for a couple of hours. Time flew by—it seems like it's been minutes, not hours. I need to get back to the house and shower.

"Come on, boy. It's time to head back to your stall."

Petting him brings us both comfort, and he lets out a sigh.

Happiness shines in the pools of his eyes. Once I get him all situated in his stall, I say goodbye and head back toward the house. Time has passed by quickly today, and if I don't hurry up and shower, I'll be late.

As soon as I walk in the backdoor I hear paper rustling in the other room. I stop in my tracks and open my senses, feeling out the signature of the person in the other room. Vampire. Opening my mind, I seek out the thoughts of said vampire. Alex. Knowing it's just my cousin, my shoulders relax.

Alex has no manners, none whatsoever. I'm not sure why I ever gave the man a key to my home; not that it really matters, since I only lock my house at night. We may be related, but that does not mean he has free reign to come and go as he pleases. Yet, I have never actually told him his intrusions were unwelcome. After all, we're family, I can't really say no, so I just keep my thoughts to myself.

I glare at the wall separating us. "What do you want? I'm in a hurry."

A rustle of paper and a soft thud where it lands on the floor is the only sound as he enters the kitchen and pulls a beer from the refrigerator. Twisting the cap, he takes a long pull from the bottle.

Isn't it a little early to be drinking? I lean my hip on the counter and cross my arms. "Dude, you own a bar. Go raid *it* and leave mine alone."

Alex chuckles then takes a seat at the table. "So, what exactly are you in a hurry for?" He raises a knowing brow, taking another swig.

"If you must know, I have a date." His smirk drives me crazy, and I'm tempted to slap it off his face. "I'm going to shower. Kindly see yourself out."

"A date, huh?" He takes another swig of his beer, propping

his feet on the chair next to him. "Would this be a date with that fine chick from the club last night?"

Those words anger me, and I'm not quite sure why. It's not the first time I've heard my cousin refer to women as chicks, babes, or hotties, but this time it's different. "Her name's Desiree, smartass."

Humor glistens in his annoying blue eyes. "Wow, I haven't seen you smitten with a girl in centuries." He tips the bottle and polishes off the last of his beer. When I don't say a word, he sets the empty bottle on the tabletop and stands. "Have fun on your date."

Even though Alex drives me insane, I love the man. Not just because he's the only family I have left, but because regardless of our differences, this man has been by my side through it all. He's seen the good, the bad, and the ugly. Blood relation aside, Alex is my best friend.

Turning the water as hot as it will go, I step into the stall and let the spray wash over my body. The heat beats down on my tense muscles, uncoiling them. Lathering soap in my hands, I wash the dirt and grime from myself and watch as it goes down the drain.

A towel is hanging on a hook near the shower stall. I grab it and begin drying myself. The shower was refreshing. It always feels like heaven after a hard day's work on the ranch. I tuck my button-up in my Wranglers and fasten my belt, adjusting the large buckle until it's straight.

Stepping out of the bathroom, I walk across my bedroom to choose shoes for this evening. There are several pairs of boots lining the floor of my closet, and I choose my only black pair. This pair is my favorite, and the tips are adorned with shiny metal. It isn't what you'd call a typical cowboy boot—its more sophisticated. Perfect for my date.

For the first time in five hundred and fifty years, I'm nervous. This feeling is foreign to me, and I can feel an inkling of butterflies in my stomach. What kind of a man gets damn butterflies in his stomach? Isn't that a girly thing? Hell, I'm falling apart at the seams.

Blood. I need blood. Surely that will calm my nerves. I open the mini fridge I keep next to my bed and pull out two bags of blood. Forget the cup—I puncture the plastic with my fangs, needing sweet relief from whatever has me on edge.

Funny thing is, I know exactly what has me on edge. Desiree. Her face invades my mind as I drink the cold blood. Her lips, so plump and inviting, taunt me, and I inhale a sharp breath. I need to quit thinking about those lips if I'm to be the gentleman that I am.

I toss the empty bag in the garbage and slap the second bag against my fangs. The two bags won't be enough to calm the beast within, so I swing open the mini fridge and grab another. Three bags later and I finally feel more like myself.

I toss the last of the empty bags in the garbage and retrieve my cell phone from my back pocket, and send a quick text to Desiree. *Fixin' to leave the house. See ya shortly, darlin'.*

Chapter Thirteen
Desiree

Reading Caleb's text, I hug the phone to my chest and squeal with excitement. My heart flutters and I get goosebumps every time I think of him. I look up in time to see Tracy roll her eyes. "Hey, missy." Jabbing a finger in her chest, I say, "This is all your fault. You dragged me to that club." And I'm so glad she did. Caleb has brought life back into my soul.

"Yeah, yeah. I know." She pats me on the back. "Don't get me wrong, I'm happy that you're finally living life." Digging a tube of lipstick from her purse, she applies color to her already cherry tinted lips. "I'm just not used to this side of you."

"Tell me about it—I feel like my high school self." I smooth my hands down the sides of my off-the-shoulder lace top. "Do I look okay? I kind of feel ridiculous."

Tracy blots her red lips on a napkin, then shoves her lipstick back in her purse, studying me with a look of admiration. "You look fabulous, Des." Tracy is the fashionista, so I'm totally relying her skills and knowledge. I hope Caleb approves. Yes, I realize I sound like a teenage girl with a major crush, but dang, that man has gotten under my skin. I hope this date leads to many, many more.

While I've been busy dressing up, so has Tracy. It's only now that I notice she is dressed to impress. "So, what, or who, are you getting all dolled up for?"

Tracy lowers her eyeliner, looking at me through the mirror. "Nothing special." She goes back to running the eyeliner along her lids. "I'm just going back to the club tonight."

Even though she is focusing on applying her makeup, I smile at her. There is something different about her. Lust shines in her eyes. Her trip to the club has nothing to do with it being a weekend and wanting to party. No, this is something else entirely. "Did you meet someone worth getting to know a little better?"

She's doing her best not to smile, but is failing miserably. "Maybe." Saying nothing else, she finishes her task of applying eyeliner and mascara.

I hear what sounds like a big truck pulling up in the driveway. Those pesky butterflies start dancing again, and I bite my lip to calm my nerves. Peeking out the window, I gasp. It's a big truck all right. Tires the size of Montana hold a black Ford so far up that I'll need a stepstool just to get in.

Caleb exits the vehicle and makes his way up the sidewalk. This man is not your average Oklahoma cowboy. Most men that dress western are nothing more than cowboy wannabes, but Caleb looks and acts just like a southern gentleman. The kind that you read about in romance novels.

As if a neon sign is blinking in my direction, his eyes veer to the right and he catches me watching from the window. The corners of his mouth lift and goosebumps break out on my flesh, causing me to shiver. His smile grows wider, like he can see the effect he has on me. I know that's absurd—he's not close enough to see me *that* clearly.

We keep eye contact until he reaches the porch. Sweat builds in my palms and I shake my hands to air dry them. How is it that Caleb can ignite this strange nervousness in me? The way I feel is not unwelcome, it's just a feeling I'm not accustomed to.

Two seconds later the doorbell rings and Tracy rushes past me, beating me to the front door. Flinging the wooden door open, she inspects him fully. "Club lights don't do you justice, boy. You are dang near the hottest guy I've ever laid eyes on."

Humor sparkles in his irises, and he chuckles. "Thanks."

"Come on in." Stepping to the side, Tracy waves him in.

Glancing over Tracy's shoulder, he looks uncertain. His feet do not move from the doormat, and I want to assure him that it's perfectly okay for him to step into my home, so I say, "Come in."

As if he's afraid of being electrocuted by entering my house, his foot inches over the threshold. Once his boot lands on the hardwood floor, the uncertainty vanishes from his face.

Fingers wrap around my arm. Tracy tugs me close to her side like a proud momma. "Good job, Des, he's a looker."

I want to crawl in a hole and hide. My friend has no filter, and I hope she doesn't run him off. If she does, I do believe I will kill her. In hopes of getting Caleb far away before she says anything stupid, I nudge her out of the way and greet Caleb with a quick hug.

His thick corded arms wrap around me, his spicy cologne warming my senses. Yep, I do believe I am currently falling in love with this man. I know I only met him last night, but it doesn't change the fact that he does something wonderful to me. I feel a deep connection with him. Crazy, I know, but I can't deny it.

"Hey there, darlin'." He hands me a crystal vase full of beautiful red and pink roses. Lifting the vase, I smell their petals. Rich and sweet. Setting the vase on the end table, I allow him to thread his fingers with mine. "You ready?"

Am I ready? Of course, I'm ready. "Yes, sir." I follow him out the door and to his vehicle.

Staring up at the truck, I wonder how in the hell I'm going to climb into that monster. A laugh escapes him, and I look at him questioningly. How is it that this man always seems to laugh at just the right moment to match what is being said in my brain? I swear, if he is a psychic and can read my mind, I'm going to dig a hole and bury myself alive.

The amusement in his eyes sure does look like he just heard that little rant I had in my head, which is not possible. *Oh, my goodness, I'm losing my ever-loving mind.* I need to quit fearing the impossible and just enjoy my time with him. The last thing I want to do is run him off.

"Come here, darlin'." He holds his hand out. "I'll hoist you up."

Taking a step toward him, he slips an arm under my knees and one at my back, lifting me bridal style into his tall truck. He lingers there a moment, tracing circles on my knee before shutting the door and taking his place behind the wheel.

As soon as he starts his truck country music blares from the speakers. He moves to turn it down, but I halt him by placing my hand over his. "Please don't, I love this song."

There's no way his smile can grow any wider, not even if he tries. Letting his hand fall, he backs out of my driveway as I sing the words to "Make You Miss Me," doing my best to harmonize with Sam Hunt. Caleb raises a brow but says nothing.

This is my all-time favorite song, and when I'm in my zone I don't care what people think, I just belt out the lyrics and let myself get lost in the music. When the song is over, I glance over at Caleb, hoping that I didn't sing horribly off key.

He turns the volume down and whistles. "Damn, darlin'." Meeting my gaze, he says, "That was the most beautiful thing I've ever heard."

I wish my singing was *that* good, but I know it's not. No matter how much I wish I could sing, I know I'm not cut out for it.

His brows furrow. "You haven't a clue, do ya?"

I shake my head in confusion. "What?"

He takes my hand in his. "Darlin', you've got a voice like an angel."

I want to believe him, but even my own music teacher in middle school told me that I wasn't cut out for singing. Hence my career choice as a nurse. Which is fine by me. I love working with the kids and helping them get well.

Chapter Fourteen
Caleb

I take Desiree to the Mexican restaurant downtown. Looking over the menu, she surprises me by ordering a fajita salad. Fajita salad—I didn't even know there was such a thing. Of course, I never look at any part of the menu aside from the combos.

My temptress is sipping on her cactus cooler, batting her eyelashes playfully at me. "You look beautiful tonight," I say.

A blush colors her cheeks, but she smirks around her straw. Setting her glass down, she licks her lips, dragging her teeth over her plump bottom lip. "Oh, I wasn't beautiful last night?"

I love that teasing tone of hers. "No, you were plenty beautiful last night." Tipping my glass, I drink my beer. Her eyes watch my Adam's apple bob with each swallow.

Wrapping her lips around her straw, she sips her drink. "So, what made you decide to go into business with your cousin if you already own a ranch?"

I can't stop the chuckle. My cousin couldn't run a successful business if he tried. I take that back, he could run a business... straight into the ground. "Alex is not a good business man. At all. Owning a club was a dream of his, and I love that crazy fool so I partnered with him so he could fulfill his desire."

Nodding, she hums an "Ah" as if she understands my

reasoning. The waiter brings our plates to the table, and the sight of her salad shocks me. It's a salad with grilled fajita meat and veggies. I would have never thought to add the two foods together. Noticing my stare, she asks, "Want a bite?"

Yes, I do, it looks very appetizing. "If you don't mind." She stabs a thick piece of chicken, bell pepper, onion, and lettuce, holding her fork in front of my face. My eyes don't stray from hers when I open my mouth to taste her salad. It's good. It's more than good, it's fantastic. The next time I come here I'm ordering one.

We eat in silence but it's not awkward silence — we're just enjoying one another's presence while we enjoy our food. I offer her a bite of my chile relleno, and in turn she gives me another bite of her salad. When our food is gone and the waiter comes to collect our plates, he asks if we would like dessert.

I give Desiree a questioning look and she shakes her head. "None for me, thank you."

After the meal I just ate, I don't have room for dessert either. "We'll take the check. Thank you."

Exiting the restaurant hand-in-hand, we walk across the street to the park and watch the sun set. Her beautiful black hair is blowing in the breeze, and she twists it then drapes it over her shoulder.

When she shivers, I offer her my jacket. It's not like I need it anyway — I'm a vampire. The temperature doesn't bother me one iota. Holding my jacket so she can slip her arms into the sleeves, I smile at the way it swallows her whole. The sleeves are way too long, and she is fighting to keep her hands out past the cuffs.

"So, what made you choose nursing as your career?"

There's a shift in the wind and her once happy and relaxed eyes grow sorrowful. Casting her gaze downward, she squirms on the bench like she's ready to bolt. If I'd known my question would cause her discomfort, I would have kept my mouth shut.

In an attempt to keep her from leaving my side, I trace the back of her hand with my forefinger. "You don't have to answer that."

Her shoulders rise with the deep breath she inhales. "It's okay." Turning her body toward me, her gaze meets mine and my heart aches at the pain I see swimming in her brown pools. "When I was in high school, my cousin, Danny, was diagnosed with cancer. He was only three." A lone tear runs down her cheek, and I swipe it away. "He underwent treatment, but it was so advanced that his little body just couldn't carry on."

I feel horrible. There is nothing worse than losing someone you love. Loss is not foreign to me; I've had hundreds of years to experience that pain, and it's not one I would wish on anybody. To lose a child? That's a pain I couldn't imagine.

Pulling a tissue from her purse, she dabs at her eyes. "My uncle Dan couldn't handle the loss." Gazing over my shoulder, she stares at something in the distance. "He drove his car off a bridge, killing himself and his wife."

Whoa. Desiree has been through more than enough turmoil to last a lifetime. Wrapping my arm around her, I pull her into my side. "I'm sorry that y'all had to go through that."

She smiles, but it doesn't quite reach her eyes. "Thank you." Straightening her spine, she lets out a long breath. "It was so long ago, but it seems like only yesterday." There's a war raging within her, and she's fighting demons that should have stayed buried.

Seeing her like this breaks me in two, and I feel like a jerk for raising her demons from the dead. I allow her the time she needs to push them back into their grave. Two minutes pass, and she finally blinks the moisture from her eyes and relaxes into my side. Now that I have her back, I relax with her and we continue to watch the sun set.

A couple runs past us and dogs bark in the distance. It's been too long since I've taken the time to sit back and enjoy nature. Yes, I live on a ranch and I'm around nature on a daily basis, but in addition to working on the ranch I help Alex operate his club. Therefore I don't get the opportunity to just sit back and enjoy the beauty that surrounds me.

The sun finally sets and the night air turns from chilly to downright cold. Desiree shivers and I stand, holding my hand out for her. It's easy for me to forget just how cold a person can get. I haven't felt the effects of the weather in nearly six hundred years.

"Come on, darlin'." She grasps my hand and I help her to her feet. "Let's get you somewhere warm." I lead her to the truck and crank up the heater; the last thing I want is for her to catch a cold. Without hesitation, she slides over and rests her head on my shoulder. The smell of her perfume wafts up and I inhale deeply, ingraining the scent to memory.

Before I pull onto the main road the heater is blasting blazing-hot air. Desiree sighs, her shivering long gone, and lets her hand rest on my knee. I love the way this feels, so natural. If she knew the truth about me, would she still want to be with me? The thought of her not wanting me scares me. Losing her is the last thing I want. This may sound insanely crazy, but I think I've finally found my soul mate.

Gentle strokes of her fingers trace circles on my knee, and I pray she doesn't notice the effect her touch has on me. "I don't want this night to end." Her voice is soft and content, which causes my heart to blossom.

"Me either, darlin'."

When her fingers slow, I glance down and see that she's fighting to keep her eyes open. I look at the clock on the dash and notice that its nearing midnight. How in the world did the night go by so quickly? It feels as though only minutes have gone by, not hours.

I continue driving around, not willing to let her go just yet. This contentedness is a welcome change to my life, and I enjoy the high it brings to my body. A few more minutes and her breathing evens out, signaling her slumber. Her body begins to sag, and I drape my arm over her to hold her in place.

As I turn onto Union Avenue, my phone dings with a text and I roll my eyes. Only one person texts me. Well, that's not entirely true. Desiree texts me, but other than her there's only one other. Alex. I remove my arm from around her and she moans in protest. Carefully I lift off the seat so I can remove my phone from my back pocket and open his message.

I think this fine babe is friends with your date. Look familiar?

Immediately, a picture comes through. Red hair spread over the counter and cherry-red lips open in sleep. Yes, I recognize her. This is the same friend that left with Desiree last night, the same one that greeted me this evening.

Typing one-handedly while driving isn't the easiest of tasks, but I manage. *Yeah, that's Desiree's friend.*

Almost immediately another text comes through. *Good. She's passed out and I have no idea where to take her.*

Since Desiree is passed out I should get her home. I fumble with my phone, trying to reply to Alex. *Meet me at Desiree's. She lives on the north corner of 7th and Bell Ave.*

Alex sends me some emoji of a thumbs up. I swear my cousin does this just to annoy the crap out of me. I toss my phone on the dash, ignoring him and his stupid emoji images.

It doesn't take long to get to Desiree's house; we weren't too far away when Alex sent that text. I pull into the driveway and gently shake her. She doesn't open her eyes, just wraps her arm around my waist and snuggles closer.

"Darlin'." I shake her again. "We're at your house. Want to hand me your keys so I can unlock your door?"

At first I don't think she's heard me, but after a minute her eyes flutter open. It takes her a second to focus on me, but once she does a huge smile adorns her face, and it warms me from the inside out.

When she sits up I get out and motion for her to slide into my waiting arms. "I've got ya, darlin'."

She hesitates, biting her lip. Good grief, if she only knew what that does to me. Reaching down and grabbing her purse, she slides out of my truck and into my waiting arms. I carry her to the door and hold my hand out when she retrieves the keys from her purse.

Once the door is unlocked, I shove it open with my foot and carry her to the couch. Before I straighten, I place a chaste kiss on her plump and oh-so-tempting lips. "Alex texted me and said your friend had passed out at the club." Her eyes widen. "I hope you don't mind, but I told him to bring her here."

Letting out a breath, she relaxes into the cushion. "No, that's perfectly fine. Thank you."

Chapter Fifteen
Desiree

Lead. That's what my eyelids feel like. I am so tired and my eyelids are droopy, but I'm putting up a good fight. The last thing I want to do is close my eyes until I know that Tracy is safe. Alex is nothing like Caleb. Where Caleb is a gentleman, Alex is conceited and shamelessly flirty. I don't trust the man as far as I can throw him, which is not at all. Alex is nothing more than a man-whore.

Ding dong. The sound of the doorbell startles me, and my heart pounds so hard I can hear it in my ears. I move to stand, but Caleb holds his hand up for me to stay put. "I got it." His hand caresses my cheek before he moves toward the door. "You go ahead and rest."

Tingles linger where his fingers were touching my skin, calming my locomotive heart. Now that the pounding of my beating organ is back to normal, I check the time on my phone. Twenty-five minutes after midnight. No wonder I'm so dang sleepy. One thing is for sure, I'm going to sleep like a rock tonight.

A click echoes in the quiet when the deadbolt turns, followed by Caleb's voice when he greets Alex. I crane my neck to see once their voices drop to hushed tones. They're so quiet I can't make out a single word that's being said.

My curiosity must be burning Caleb's ears, because he looks over his shoulder, those gorgeous hazel eyes locking with mine. Tenderness shines bright in those hazel pools, along with something else I can't quite decipher.

Alex's gaze turns to me. "Well, Sunshine, can I come in?"

I find it odd that he asks me this question while holding my best friend in his arms. Caleb is holding the door wide open; why doesn't he just step inside? "Of course you can come in."

He steps into the room with Tracy draped over his shoulder like a sack of potatoes. When he is standing in front of me, his lips turn up into a cocky smile and he's practically undressing me with his eyes.

Ugh, creep.

Patting Tracy's rear, he says, "Where do you want me to put her?"

The man has no shame. If I weren't so exhausted, I'd cross the room and slap the turd for manhandling my best friend. Fortunately for him, I don't have the strength to stand, let alone exert enough energy to pop his face with my hand, so I settle for instructions. Pointing toward the hallway, I say, "Oh, my bedroom is down the hall. Just tuck her into the bed."

Amusement crosses his features and he raises a brow. "Your room, huh?" Waggling those brows, a purr rumbles low in his throat. "Kinky. I like it."

Kinky? Oh, Lord, help him. Rolling my eyes, I ignore his sex starved comment. Some men just have no class, and Alex is one of the worst I have seen. Thank God Caleb is nothing like him. I can't believe they're even related.

The door shuts with enough force the sound bounces off the walls. Caleb walks into the living room shaking his head, and swears under his breath. "Just ignore him. He's a prick."

Oh, believe me, I will. "Already have." I smile to let him

know I'm unaffected by his idiotic cousin. "I think he might have been dropped on his head as a baby," I say loud enough for Alex to hear.

"Hey. I'm deeply wounded." Alex waltzes back into the room, one hand tucked into his front pocket and the other covering his heart. "Your words sting my heart, Sunshine."

I roll my eyes. "Sunshine?"

One side of Alex's lips curve up. "What, would you rather I call you babe?"

I shake my head. "I'd rather you not call me anything other than Desiree."

Alex grunts at my confession. "Fine, Desiree it is. At least until you come to your senses and become my babe."

I'll never be his anything.

Pointing his thumb behind him, Alex says, "She's all tucked in and snoring like a freight train."

"Rude." Though a freight train is a pretty accurate description of Tracy's snores. That girl could wake the dead with her funky snoring.

"Have you heard that woman?" Alex jams his thumb in the direction of my bedroom, again. "She'd scare a bear in the wilderness with that commotion."

It takes a great amount of effort not to laugh. Biting the inside of my cheek, I continue to give him a hard time. "Are you positive that he's your blood relative?" I ask Caleb. "Maybe he was actually adopted."

The laugh that expels from Caleb rings throughout the room. "I ask myself that all the time. I'm dang-near positive he was switched at birth."

The frown that forms on Alex's face is priceless. "You two are such a joy to be around." With an eye roll, he heads for the door. "I have better things to do than stand here and listen to

76

your insults."

I watch as Caleb walks his cousin to the door. The hug they give each other shows their bond is stronger than their sibling-like rivalry. Standing in the doorway, the two of them have a quiet discussion. Curiosity makes me wish I could hear what they're saying, but I don't know either of them well enough to be a nosey body.

After they've said their goodbyes, the door closes and the sound of Caleb's footsteps echoes in the all-to-quiet house. His black boots stop in front of me and I look up into his captivating hazel eyes. "Darlin', you need some sleep."

I shake my head. The last thing I want is for him to leave. Yes, I'm exhausted, but I'm not ready to part with him just yet. His shoulders shake with silent laughter. "Hey, don't laugh at me."

He sits next to me. "I'll stay for a bit." Draping his arm over my shoulders, he pulls me into his side. "Go ahead and close your eyes. I've got ya."

I've got ya. Those three words ring over and over in my head. Being in his arms like this feels like home. For the first time in my life I feel like I belong. I feel safe. I feel loved.

Chapter Sixteen
Caleb

Soft snoring fills the room, and I stroke Desiree's hair from her face. I'm not a fan of noisy sleepers, but coming from her, it's music to my ears. It sounds stupid, but it's the truth. There is something about her that resonates with my soul. I feel so at peace with her lying in my arms like this.

As crazy as it may be. I do believe that she is my forever. Yes, even so soon after we met. There's not a chance in hell I will mention this to Alex. My cousin has never even dated the same woman twice. If he catches wind that I want to share the rest of my life with Desiree after just one day, he'll hit me over the head with a baseball bat.

A sigh escapes Desiree, and immediately following is a grin. Must be some dream she's having. Watching her sleep is something I could do all night. I know I should carry her to bed so she can get a good night's rest, but I just can't bring myself to part with her yet. The thought of leaving her pains me.

Maybe I'll just be a selfish SOB and sit here with her sprawled across my lap until the sun rises. The weight of her body and the feel of her skin is heaven, and I'm not ready to break this contact. My fingers trace the lines of her face, lowering to her lips. Gentle strokes of my fingers smooth along her bottom lip, and I want so badly to lean over and wake her with a kiss.

The stress lines that marred her beautiful forehead earlier tonight are now gone. Thank God. Knowing I was the one that put them there by bringing up bad memories made me feel like a heel. A puff of air hits my finger where it's still tracing her bottom lip. She's sleeping peacefully, her eyelids twitching every now and then with the movement of her eyes. Another smile lifts the corners of her mouth, and I wish I knew what she was dreaming. Whatever it is, it's making her happy, and in turn that makes my heart soar.

Ding. Why is Alex texting my blasted phone at this hour? He knows where I am. Carefully, I lift my body so I can retrieve my cell phone from my back pocket. A quick glance down at her confirms that she didn't wake with my movements.

This had better be good or he and I will go to fist-city. Tapping the message icon, I read the text from Alex.

Did you stop by the club and empty out the blood in the back fridge?

What? I went to the club earlier, but it was to go over the books and to place an order for more liquor. A chill gradually seeps into my bones, leaving goosebumps on my flesh. Someone has been helping themselves to our blood, and it's not sitting right with me. I type a response. *No, I didn't.*

Before my screen can timeout, it dings again. *That's odd. I could have sworn that I filled it earlier today. Maybe I'm mistaken.*

That's more than odd. Alex doesn't make mistakes like that. When it comes to our blood supply he's OCD. This whole situation reeks of foul play. I just wish I could solve this puzzle before things take a turn for the worse.

Only two keys exist to that back room. His key and mine. *Has anyone else been back there tonight?*

Alex must have his phone in hand because as soon as I send the text, his response immediately follows. *No. It's been locked up tight. No worries, I must have misplaced the cooler of blood and just thought I stocked up.*

No, absolutely not. There is no way that Alex misplaced a cooler of blood. The moment it arrived he would have stocked the back fridge. Now, if it had been me then I could see the possibility of misplacement, but for him to misplace it, there's no way in hell that happened.

My fingers tap the glass screen as I type. *You sure about that? You didn't let Phil back there or leave your keys lying on the counter?* I know he would never leave his keys out in the open with a club full of patrons, but I have to cover every angle.

Yes, I'm positive. My keys have not left my possession.

Things are not adding up. Since the day we opened the club, we have not had one issue with theft. Rather than pushing him further on the subject, I think I'll just let him be. For now, anyway. Come tomorrow, I fully intend to find out what happened to that blood. *We'll get this worked out when I get back over there.*

Damn right, we will. Good night, Caleb.

Night, Alex.

Tapping the corner of my cell phone on the arm of the couch, I mull over our conversation. The same creepy feeling I got last night consumes me again, crawling under my skin like a parasite. Something wicked is coming this way, and I think this missing blood is somehow connected.

The more I dwell on the issue, the more my skin crawls. This wicked feeling that's washing over me seems all too familiar. Deep in my gut I know the reason why my body's warning alarm is blaring, but I can't bring myself to believe it. There's no way he could be here. Alex and I took care of that problem five hundred years ago.

Chapter Seventeen
Desiree

Stabbing pain radiates through my neck. Oh man, it hurts something fierce. Did I fall asleep on the couch with my head at an odd angle? A groan vibrates from my throat and I slowly open my dry eyes, blinking to bring moisture back into them. Just as I thought, I'm on the couch and my neck is bent in an awkward position.

Needing to get up and stretch my aching muscles and bones, I lean forward, but an arm slips around me, pulling my body back down. This act alarms me and my eyes open wide, my hands reaching for the arm around me as I crane my neck to focus on the person holding me captive. Caleb. I let out a relieved breath.

Body upright and head twisted to the side, Caleb is sleeping. The muscles in his arm relax now that my movements have ceased. My lips turn upward at his possessive hold on my body. I fully expected to wake in my own bed and find Caleb gone. But he didn't leave, he stayed overnight. This is what I have always imagined being in a relationship would be like. Falling asleep in each other's arms. *This.* I could easily get used to this.

Admiring him is easy while he's asleep. I can take my time memorizing every crease, every dimple. Dark brown strands of hair stick up on one side of his head, most likely from running his hand through it at one point in the night. Very slowly I lean up, careful not to disturb him. An overwhelming need to kiss his oh-so-tempting lips is driving me forward.

Gently, as to not wake him, I press my lips against his. Those smooth lips of his are soft and warm. One kiss will not be enough. My hand rests on his cheek as I plant another kiss to those irresistible lips of his. The arm around my waist shifts, and I find myself being hoisted to straddle his lap.

The sudden movement startles me and I open my eyes. His eyes are on me, and they're ten shades darker than normal. Staring into that hooded gaze raises my body temperature. The desire stirring in me matches what I see in his gaze.

Opening his mouth, his tongue darts out, seeking permission, and I am all too willing to grant him access. Our tongues chase each other, dancing and caressing. Desire ignites a spark in my belly that soon bursts into flames. My breathing escalates and my skin is crying out for his touch.

Of their own accord, my hips start rocking against his and a moan gets caught in my throat. Oh, this feels good. I rock with a little more force, and Caleb's moan matches mine. My hands slide up his chest, wrapping around his neck. His grip on me tightens, his fingers digging into my hip. After two nights of knowing this man, I'm ready to give myself to him. This is what I want, what my body wants. What kind of woman does that make me? I need to slow this down—I'm not emotionally ready for the next level. Heck, I'm not even sure how many women he's been with. I could end up with an STD or something. Eww. That's a talk we need to have before I strip naked and give myself to him. Besides, I'm not on birth control, nor do I own a single condom. *Crap, I need to rein in my horny-teenage-acting emotions before I get myself in trouble.*

All too soon, Caleb breaks our kiss. He leans back, smiles at me, and gives me a peck on the nose. "Mornin'."

"Good morning." My words come out breathless and I'm already missing his mouth on mine. Tightening his hold on me, he stands with me in his arms and carries me to the kitchen, where he sets me on the countertop. Without saying a word, he opens the cupboard and takes out the box of K-cups and a coffee mug.

While the Keurig is brewing the coffee, he gets out the bacon and eggs. Watching him move about my kitchen, caring for me, brings me such joy. Other than a restaurant, the last time anyone cooked for me was when I was a teenager living at home. I want to tell him that I'm glad he stayed the night, but I don't want to sound like a needy idiot.

His shoulders shake and I know he is soundlessly laughing. How does he manage to laugh at the exact same time as the mini meltdowns in my head? Instead of saying anything, I swing my legs and patiently wait for my coffee.

After arranging several strips of bacon into the pan, he washes his hands and then brings me the cup of coffee. "Here ya go, darlin'."

Steam rises from the cup and I inhale the heavenly aroma. *Mmm.* "Thank you."

He taps the end of my nose. "There's no need to thank me. It's my pleasure." Returning to the stove, he cracks the eggs. They pop and sizzle under the heat of the pan. The scents of bacon and eggs mingle together in the air, wafting toward me, and my stomach rumbles at the scent. If they don't hurry and cook, I may have to eat them raw.

I take a sip and the coffee burns my tongue. The sting causes me to wince. Normally I wait until it cools a bit, but this morning I seem to be slightly distracted by the sight in front of me. Sucking in a breath to cool my aching tongue, I rest the coffee cup on my knee. "Tell me about your ranch. Do you have farm animals?"

Glancing over his shoulder, then back to his task, he says, "I have cows, pigs, and some chickens." He turns the bacon over and flips the eggs. "And I own a few horses."

"I've always wanted a horse." Lifting my cup, I blow then take a sip. The coffee is still blazing hot, but I'm in need of caffeine. "I got to ride a horse once when I went to summer camp. I fell in love with her and wanted my own, but Grandma didn't have the money or land to get one."

Piling food on the three plates, he sticks one in the microwave and brings the other two to the table. "Well, we'll have to fix that then, won't we?" He holds his hand out and helps me off the counter.

Unsure of how to respond to his last statement, I keep silent. I mean, does he actually want me at his ranch or is he just being polite? This is the south, everyone is polite, but just because they say "Hey, you ought to come see my ranch," doesn't necessarily mean they want you to go hang out at their place.

The breakfast he cooked was simply bacon and fried eggs, but it is the best home cooked meal I've had in a long time. Jeez, I must be falling in love if I consider bacon and fried eggs the best home cooked meal.

Footsteps sound in the hallway, and I turn to see Tracy stomping about with a head full of tangles. She rubs her eyes and glares in my direction, not necessarily at me. "I need coffee, stat." Without asking, she picks up my mug and gulps it down, moaning in satisfaction.

"I left you a plate in the microwave." Caleb points his fork toward the appliance.

Clearly startled, Tracy jumps and fumbles to gain control over my coffee mug. "Des, why didn't you tell me that you had company? I would have at least brushed my hair." She runs her fingers through it in a vain attempt to tame the wild locks.

84

It doesn't take her long to zero in on our plates and forget about her hair. Drawing in a breath, she rubs her growling belly. Rushing to the microwave, she snatches her plate out and shovels eggs into her mouth as she walks toward the table. Manners seem to be lost on her for the moment, and I giggle at her.

"When do you go back to work?"

Caleb directs his question at me, but Tracy answers it for the both of us. "Tuesday."

His hand reaches across the table and rests on mine. "How would you feel about visiting the ranch overnight?"

Tracy points her fork at me. "Go. You need a day or two of wild monkey sex to relieve all that tension."

I'm taken aback by her bluntness. Her words bring heat to my cheeks, and I hope Caleb doesn't get the wrong impression of me. Sex is not something I give away so easily, though my actions this morning show the exact opposite. "Tracy, what gives?"

With a mouth full of food, she giggles. "What? How long has it been anyway — our first semester in college?"

I want to crawl under the table and dig my way to China.

"So, what do ya say, darlin'? Will you come home with me?"

Either he's deaf or he is ignoring my best friend. It doesn't matter which, I'm grateful he isn't running for the hills. After the garbage that came out of Tracy's mouth, I'm happy he still wants me to go home with him. "I'd love to, but I have Mittens to take care of."

Caleb glances down at the cat that is currently curling around his feet. "Oh, I think she'll get along just fine at the ranch."

I open my mouth to say something when his words finally register. "Did you just offer to bring my cat with us?"

He wipes his mouth on a napkin and takes our dishes to the sink. "I did."

Mittens meows, stretches her front legs, and walks circles

around Caleb's feet. Looks like my cat is just as smitten with the man as I am.

"She'd love to," Tracy says with a mouth full of eggs.

"Good. Then its settled." Bending over, he picks up my cat then scratches her behind the ear. "You're coming home with me."

Chapter Eighteen
Caleb

I'm so glad that Desiree agreed to come home with me. That nagging feeling of impending doom scares me out of my wits for her safety. Thoughts of her untimely death fill my conscious mind, and it has me insane with worry. After all, she's a defenseless mortal, and I don't plan on allowing evil to take her from me.

Turning right onto River Road, gravel crunches under my tires and Desiree inhales sharply. The sign straight ahead says Southern Shade Ranch, and the small dirt driveway stretches on for half a mile to the house.

"This is your ranch?" Her mouth is hanging open in what appears to be shock.

"Yep." I park the truck in front of the house and unload her bags.

After I help her down, she scoops up her cat and points to my house. "That's not a house. That is a friggin' mansion." She looks at me with her wide eyes. "I could fit four of my houses inside that thing."

Her house is small, yes, but what she doesn't understand is that I don't live alone. My house is large because I've added on to it over the years to accommodate my help and my wants and needs. I can't help but laugh at her exclamation. "It hasn't always

87

been this big. My dad built the front portion of the house, I've just added on to it over the years."

Mittens jumps from her arms and walks around my ankles, rubbing her head on my calves. I scoop her up, take Desiree's bags, and nod for her to follow me to the front door. She raises her brow when I open the door. "You don't keep it locked?"

An unlocked door is the norm for me; I forget how she might be used to keeping things locked up tight. "I have ranch hands that live here with me. I don't keep it locked since someone is always on the property." Then I point to the cameras at each end of the porch. "And I have plenty of surveillance."

That seems to pacify her and she enters the house, taking in the sight before her. I set her bags next to the staircase and show her around the first floor. Just inside the entryway is the living room, and across from that is the library. On either side of the staircase is a hallway. The hallway to the right leads to four bedrooms and two bathrooms for the ranch hands. The other leads to the kitchen, dining room, and laundry room.

I lead her up the stairs and to the left, the north wing, where the three guest rooms are. Each room has an adjoining bathroom and walk-in closet. Her eyes are wide as she takes in her surroundings. Pointing toward the south wing, she asks, "What's on the other side?"

"My bedroom, office, and kitchen are located on the south wing."

If her eyes grow any wider they'll fall from their sockets. "You have a wing to yourself, and it includes a kitchen?"

I'm not sure why her shock amuses me, but it does. To avoid the laughter that is bubbling up, I bite the inside of my cheek. "Yes."

"Dang." She stands still for a minute, staring toward my wing, digesting everything she's seen and heard. "Which room am I staying in?"

"Whichever you'd like." If it were up to me she'd be staying in my room, sleeping in my bed. However, I will be a gentleman about it and let her make up her own mind about where she'll be sleeping.

She opens each door and inspects the rooms. Each room has a different theme. Rustic, vintage, and modern. After looking at them twice, she settles for the modern. "I like this one."

I smile at her choice in rooms. The modern theme is my favorite out of the three. "I'll let you settle in. Feel free to utilize the dresser and the closet." I deposit her bags on the bed. "I'll be in my wing if you need me." I leave her to unpack and head to my room, a black ball of fur chasing after me.

As I push my door open, Mittens rushes in and jumps onto my dresser, purring. For some odd reason, Desiree's cat has attached herself to me. The bloomin' thing follows me everywhere I go. I love animals, don't get me wrong, but I've never really been a cat person. I prefer horses. Cats shed on everything and are shamelessly selfish, unlike my horses, who are unselfish and gentle souls.

Knock, knock.

I make my way to the bedroom door. Desiree is standing on the other side, twirling a strand of hair around her perfect little finger. "Hi."

The way she's biting her lip is intoxicating to my soul. It's the sexiest damn thing I have ever seen. She's either oblivious to the effect it has on me or she enjoys my torment. *Behave, Caleb. Remember, you brought her here to see the animals, not to lay claim to her body.* "Would you like to see the horses?"

A smile curves her lips. My word, I love the way her face lights up when she's happy. "Yes, please."

On our way to the stable, Desiree stops to smell the roses.

I have several rose bushes along the way, and she is weaving her way through them, admiring their beauty. "I love roses." She bends to smell one of the pink tipped roses. "Mmm, they smell so good."

"I think so too." I allow her time to admire the flowers, and when she's ready we walk hand-in-hand to the stable.

Badger hears us enter and starts making noise. I scratch his jaw and he leans his head into my hand, hungry for my attention. Desiree is twisting her hands together. I can tell that she is eager to pet him, but apprehensive.

"Go ahead."

At my encouragement, she steps forward and pets his face. When he tilts his head toward her, she smiles and gives him her full attention. "Aren't you the cutest thing in the world?" Seems she's fallen in love with my horse, and him with her. If I'm not careful, he will adopt her as his new owner. Honestly, I wouldn't mind that happening if it means Desiree joins my family.

Once she has gotten to know Badger, I saddle up the horses, helping her up onto my horse, and take her out for a ride. The joy on her face is priceless. It's clear to see that moments like this are rare for her, and that breaks my heart. Life should be more than hard work. Relaxation should be a normal part of life, and I will do everything in my power to ensure she gets moments like this on a regular basis.

Chapter Nineteen
Desiree

I never knew how tranquil riding a horse could be. Riding Badger in a secluded part of the ranch, I'm free from the worries of this world, even if only for a little while. The only commotion facing me is the sound of birds chirping and frogs croaking at the pond's edge. A contented sigh leaves my lips. This is the life I've always wanted. Out in the middle of nowhere, no pesky neighbors, just me and nature...and of course, now I have to include Caleb.

Hooves cease thumping as Badger comes to a stop. I scratch a spot behind his ear, earning me a satisfied grunting noise.

"He seems taken with ya."

Meeting Caleb's stare, I smile. "I'm quite taken with him as well."

The smile curving his lips catches my breath. Dark hair blows into his face with the force of the breeze. My fingers itch to smooth those strands back, but he's out of my reach. His hand inches up to brush the hairs from his face, and those hazel eyes sparkle at me.

The air around me suddenly feels thin as I memorize this beautiful man beside me. With our mocha pigmented skin, his hazel eyes and square jaw, along with my straight nose and plump lips, I bet we'd have the cutest little babies. I don't know why I'm thinking such thoughts—it's not like we're a serious couple. We have only been on one official date.

Swallowing the large lump that has now formed in my throat, I mentally kick myself. *I'm such a moron.*

Cocking his head to the side and furrowing his brows, Caleb shakes his head. "You're not a moron."

Huh? Did I say that out loud? Heat scorches my cheeks and I turn my head to hide my embarrassment from him.

The sound of him sliding off his horse is the only noise I hear before his worn brown boots come into my view. He holds his hand out and I allow him to help me down. Large hands cup my face and my eyes meet his. Tapping my forehead, he asks, "What's going on in that pretty little head of yours that makes you think you're a moron?"

I breathe easier, knowing he hadn't heard all my cute baby talk. The last thing I want is for him to know I'm already having babies with him in my mind. Shaking my head, I kiss his cheek. "Nothing, I promise. I'm a woman. Sometimes I just have silly thoughts. That's all."

His grip on my face firms. Glancing at my lips then back into my eyes, he tilts my head before bringing his mouth to mine for a chaste kiss. "No more calling yourself a moron. Ya hear me?"

His words are final, there's no room for argument. "Yes, sir."

All too soon his hands leave my face, and then he helps me back onto Badger before climbing back onto his horse. "You know, it's okay to fantasize about the things your heart desires." His eyes are intensely gazing into mine. "For instance, I look at your straight nose and plump lips, and wonder what our babies will look like."

My mouth drops open and I can't close it. It's just hanging wide open, an invitation to all flying creatures to come make a home inside my mouth. I swear this man can hear my every thought.

A smirk pulls at his lips and he nods in the direction of his house. "Come on, darlin'. It's startin' to get downright chilly."

I'm still stunned speechless, but gather my hold on the reins and follow him back to the stables. Other than my embarrassing moment, today has been the best day of my life. I've seen the pigs, they stink to high heaven. The chickens were adorable, even the one that tried to peck my leg to death.

I don't know how Caleb does it. There is no way that I would be able to feed those animals, care for them, and then slaughter them for food. My heart is too sensitive for that kind of lifestyle. I'd be the one naming them Wilber, then registering them for animal exhibits to show off their talent.

The backdoor is standing wide open when we ascend the steps. Baritone voices drift over the threshold. At first it startles me, then I remember Caleb telling me about his workers that live here. Interlocking my fingers with his, I follow him through the door.

Four men are sitting at the kitchen table, a beer in hand, chatting about chores for tomorrow. At the sound of our footsteps they all turn around. A dirty-blond lifts his beer in greeting. "Hey." The rest of them mimic the first guy.

Caleb wraps his arm around my waist, tugging me into his side. "Guys, this is Desiree. Desiree, this is Mike, Billy, David, and Joe." Mike is the one with the dirty-blond hair.

"Hey." I shake their hands. They all seem sweet, but also look kind of scary. I definitely do not want to get on their bad side. Each one of them have huge muscles from working on the ranch, and look like they could lift a house with their bare hands.

"There's plenty if you two wanna join us for dinner," Joe says.

I'm not opposed to dinner with these four men, but I'm looking forward to my time with Caleb. To my relief Caleb shakes his head. "Thanks, but we're gonna head on up and have dinner."

"Okay." Joe smiles at me. "It was nice meeting you, Desiree."

"It was nice meeting you guys as well."

***

Fresh from the shower, I riffle through my bags for something comfy to wear. I am so glad that Tracy bought me some amazing outfits yesterday. I would be mortified if Caleb saw me in the worn-out shirts and faded pants that are hanging in my closet.

I pull on a pair of black jeans and a blue scarf-neck halter top. Now the question is, do I want to put on my socks and shoes or go barefoot? I hate wearing shoes. The enclosure drives me nuts—I prefer to give my toes freedom. Barefoot it is.

The carpet is thick and plush. I love the way it hugs my toes as I walk the distance to Caleb's wing. It's like walking on a giant cotton ball. Regardless of the price, this is the kind of carpet I need to purchase for my house.

As I pass the staircase and enter the south wing, the butterflies return tenfold. Little beads of sweat line my forehead. The closer I get, the more nervous I get. This is completely ridiculous—I just spent the entire day with the man. What's there to be nervous about?

The aroma from his kitchen wafts toward me and my mouth waters. Steak. I follow the scent and find Caleb standing at the stove in nothing but a pair of jeans, his hips bouncing in rhythm to the song coming from the speaker above the refrigerator.

I lean against the doorframe and watch as he dances, the muscles in his back flexing with his movements.

"It's just about ready, darlin'."

How in the world does he know that I'm here? I look around

for a monitor or mirror but there aren't any, and he hasn't looked in my direction once, so I'm baffled as to how he knew that I was standing here watching. "How did you know I was here?"

Pulling two plates down from the cupboard, he glances at me. "I could sense your presence."

Sense my presence? If I wasn't convinced before that he's psychic, I am now. That's the only explanation that makes sense. His shoulders shake with quiet laughter. This is the behavior that has me convinced he's psychic and can read my damn mind.

He sets our plates on the table. Steak, asparagus, and baked potatoes. Just the sight of it makes my mouth water. It has been years since I had a good steak. I watch as he pours wine into our glasses. This man treats me like a queen.

Holding his hand out, he beckons me to join him and I do. The steak is perfect, juicy and bursting with flavor. Each bite melts in my mouth. Next time I get a hankering for steak I'm calling Caleb to cook for me. Best. Steak. Ever.

Now I'm sitting on his couch, my head resting on his shoulder, watching *The Originals*. "Being a vampire would be amazing." His brows arch at my statement, and I hope he doesn't think I'm a lunatic. "You know, to live for eternity and never age."

That seems to have calmed his earlier concern. "Ah, yes. To be forever young." He runs the tip of his finger along my jaw. "Would that really be a life you'd want?"

A giggle rises up and bursts out of me before I can stop it. "Well, they're not real, so that question doesn't actually apply."

"Maybe." He shifts so that we're facing one another. "But if they were real, would you want an immortal life?"

"It depends." My gaze trails back toward the television. "If I could heal the sick with my blood, then yes." I spend my days around sick children, if I could heal them with a drop of my blood then I'd absolutely become a vampire. Those poor kids don't deserve a life filled with pain and suffering.

He cocks his head. "Interesting."

"Would you?"

Furrowing his brows, he asks, "Would I what, darlin'?"

"Would you become a vampire?" I'm curious, what can I say.

He worries his bottom lip before answering. "Yes, I would."

Interesting. I want to press for more, but guys generally don't like discussing this particular topic with women. So, instead I return my gaze back to the television and finish watching my show.

Chapter Twenty
Caleb

Of all the shows this woman could pick to watch, she chooses vampires. Vampires. How ironic. Her earlier admission still plays over and over in my head. "If I could heal the sick with my blood, then yes." My heart went soaring with hope when she spoke those words. Then with serious eyes, she asks, "Would you become a vampire?" It took everything in me not to chuckle.

If only she knew.

Yes, on the surface, vampirism looks appealing to her, the thought of immortality and healing the sick, but would she actually choose this life if given the chance? That's the real question. As for me, I'd be more than thrilled to have her join me in my eternal life.

The credits roll and soft snoring meets my ears, signaling that she's fallen asleep watching her show. I hit the power button on the remote to shut off the television, and shift my body so that I'm lying on the couch with her body stretched out and draped over mine. Her fruity scented hair tickles my nose and I brush the strands away.

In all honesty, I would rather take her to my bed and cuddle up with her there. It's strange, because I've never had the urge to spoon with a female companion before, but with her its damn

97

near irresistible. This woman calls out to my heart and soul like a siren's song, and my body all-too-eagerly runs toward her with open arms.

Though my heart craves every inch of her body, my consciousness overrides all my emotional desires. The last thing I want is for her to wake up in my bed only to think that I'm trying to take advantage of her. That fear is the only thing keeping me rooted to this sofa, and not hefting her in my arms and taking her to the one place I wish to have her.

No matter how badly I crave her in my bed, I refuse to put her there until she is good and ready. With Desiree, everything is different. Does my body lust for her? Hell yes, it does. But my heart seeks a connection far greater than the physical one my manhood does.

Her warm breath blows in the crook of my neck and her arms come up to cradle my head. A sigh of contentment escapes her as she snuggles closer. Curiosity has me wondering what dream is playing in her mind. Is she dreaming of me? I know I dreamed of her last night.

As tempting as it would be to probe her mind and listen in on her dreaming thoughts, I refrain. Allowing her privacy while she's sleeping is important to me. Lord knows, I wouldn't be happy finding out that Alex or some other vampire was listening in on my dreams.

The sound of my cell phone dinging in the other room draws my attention away from her. Two, three, four text messages come through. Alex knows I'm with Desiree, he wouldn't be blowing up my phone if it wasn't urgent. I carefully slip out from under Desiree and trek to my bedroom, quietly closing the door behind me.

Ding. Ding. Ding. Three more texts. I open the message icon and scroll to the top of the long list of texts from my cousin.

There was a body found a mile from the club, torn to shreds.
The police suspect a wild animal is on the loose.
You and I both know this isn't an animal attack.
There's another body. This one is at my friggin' club, on the friggin'
steps.

These messages do not sit well with me. I've had a bad feeling for a couple of days now. The missing blood, the dead bodies. There is a rogue vampire on the loose, and he, or she, seems to be targeting my cousin. But why?

The next message is a picture of the woman on his club steps, a gaping hole in her chest where her heart should be. Why would a vampire want to rip out a woman's heart? What purpose would that serve? There's plenty of blood surrounding the body, so whoever did this is not sating their hunger, they are after attention.

Clicking out of the picture, I scroll to the next message—it's another picture. I zoom in so I can see it clearly. Carved into her forehead are two lightning bolts forming an X. In the center of the X is a small D.

A gasp leaves me as I stare at the symbol on the woman's forehead. "Impossible." There is no possible way he could be the culprit. Flicking my finger on the screen, I scroll to read the final message.

Either we have an admirer on our hands or all hell is about to break
loose.

That's the understatement of the year. Moving my fingers over the screen, I send Alex a reply. *I agree with that statement one hundred percent. Though, I sincerely hope it's not the latter.*

Anger and fear well up in me at the sight of the Xavier emblem. If we are indeed dealing with an admirer, we need to find them and take them to the council for judgement. Their actions are nothing short of criminal, and their use of the emblem deserves a life sentence.

If by chance we are not dealing with an admirer...we're royally screwed.

Chapter Twenty-One
Desiree

It's been a month since I met Caleb, and since then we've been inseparable. He comes to my house every evening when I leave work and cooks dinner for me, staying until I absolutely have to get in bed. Every Friday I pack up and spend the weekend with him on the ranch. Mittens loves his house, and has claimed his bed as her own. Lucky cat.

These last few weeks have been the best days of my life. He is such a gentleman. Always holding the door open for me, pushing my chair in after I sit down, never seeking sex. I'm happy that he wants me for more than my body, but I wouldn't mind a night of passionate sex either. It's been *way* too long, and a girl has needs too.

Leaving him every Tuesday morning is the hardest thing in the world for me to do. I love my job, but I love being with Caleb more. He brightens my world. If I'm being honest, I can't imagine my life without him. A silly thing to say this early in our relationship, but it's true.

Is it possible to fall in love so quickly?

If my grandmother heard me say those words she'd slap me and tell me to straighten up before she takes me to fist-city. Maybe I am foolish for thinking that Caleb and I are meant for each other. There are loads of things we still need to learn about one another. Who can say for certain if this is love? All I know is that he is the one person I can picture myself growing old with, maybe even having children with.

Parking in front of the brick building, I inhale a cleansing breath and shut off the engine. It's been a week since I stepped foot inside Highland Nursing Home, and a wave of guilt washes over me. I know my grandma understands that I'm busy, but she doesn't deserve being neglected like this. I should be here to see her every day, even if only for fifteen minutes at a time.

The nursing staff greets me as I walk in. "Hey, Desiree." Kelly, the LPN on duty, waves at me. "Granny is in the activity room telling everyone that you're a superhero in scrubs."

"Oh boy." I wish my grandma wouldn't make up stories about me to the nursing staff and residents. I roll my eyes and Kelly laughs.

I trek down the hallway to the activity room and find my grandma wheeling her chair around the room, talking animatedly about her superhero-nurse-granddaughter. When she turns her chair around, she sees me standing in the doorway. "There's my baby girl." Pointing a slightly crooked finger in my direction, she says, "Well, what are ya waitin' for? Get on over here and take me to my room."

"Yes, Granny." I wave at the residents as I make my way across the room. "How are you?"

She pats my hand. "I'm good now that you're here."

I wheel her out of the room and to the other side of the building. She doesn't miss an opportunity to tell everyone we pass that I'm her granddaughter. They know who I am—I'm here all the time. I park her wheelchair next to a cushioned seat in the corner of her room. "I missed you."

"That's 'cause you ain't spent no time with me this week."

102

She's not disappointed in me, just stating a fact.

"I know, Granny, and I'm sorry about that."

She rests her hand on my knee. "Ain't nothin' to be sorry for; just don't forget where your priorities lie."

Time is not something I have a lot of. I have to be at the hospital in thirty minutes, so my visit with her today is going to be a brief one. During my short time with Grandma, we talk about the weather, Tracy, and Mittens. In turn, she tells me about the residents here. Bob has a great granddaughter that was born Saturday. Darla has been diagnosed with cancer. Edward left and moved to a home closer to his family.

"So, you know how I told you that I've been dating this guy?"

Grandma nods her head but doesn't say anything.

"Well, I think I'm finally falling in love."

Grandma gasps and claps her hand over her heart. "Desiree, honey, you need to be careful. You can't just go fallin' in love with just any ol' Joe."

"Oh, don't worry, Grandma." I turn my chair so that I'm facing her. "He's a perfect gentleman."

"Perfect gentleman or not, I just don't want you gettin' serious with anyone right now." She opens her mouth but closes it. There's a look in her eye like she wants to divulge something but is afraid to do so. Instead, she glances over at her nightstand, where three framed photos sit. One photo is of me with Tracy when we graduated nursing school. One is of my mom and Aunt Deidra. The other is of my uncle Dan and his wife, Aunt Trix. "Just promise me that you'll not get serious. Someday you'll understand where this old lady is comin' from."

There is no way I can promise this. I'm already head-over-heels for Caleb. I smile instead. "I gotta go. My shift starts in ten minutes."

She's not happy about my evasion, but she smiles and kisses

my cheek.

***

I'm looking over the charts when a young woman rounds the corner with a small baby in her arms and tears streaking down her cheeks. The poor boy looks malnourished and frail. I stand from my cushiony chair and walk toward her. Using her shoulder, she dries her cheeks as best she can. The nurse she's with steps forward and hands me a few papers. "He was admitted downstairs."

Looking down at the papers in my hand, I read the notes written by the admitting nurse. This boy has Prader-Willi syndrome and is suffering complications. The mother wipes her nose on her shirtsleeve. "He's been having problems sucking from his bottle. Please, help my baby."

Nodding in understanding, I take the baby from her and head toward an empty room. Holding him gently, because I'm afraid I'll break his frail little body, I smile down at him. His tiny eyes loll to the side, but eventually they look at me. Tiny and frail, this little boy is a lady killer. One side of his mouth turns up when I say, "Hey there, handsome."

I spend the rest of my shift with Elijah and his mother, getting them settled before I head back out to finish logging my charts.

The sound of Tracy clearing her throat behind me startles me, and I nearly jump out of my chair. She reaches around me to place her patient chart in the rack. "Hey, what's weighing on your mind?" She wiggles her eyebrows. "It wouldn't happen to be a hot and sexy cowboy, now would it?"

Words fail to leave my mouth, and she grins from ear-to-ear. Ignoring her, I finish making notes in the chart sitting in front of me and place it in the rack. This day has dragged on for what seems like forever. Two minutes, and then I can clock out and head home to change. Caleb will be at my house in an hour for dinner.

"Girl, you've got it bad." Tracy takes a seat next to me and turns on the computer. She clicks the icon with the hospital logo and clocks out.

"Shush." Waiting for her to move so I can clock out is like waiting on a turtle to run a race.

"Did you guys," she looks around then lowers her voice, "have wild monkey sex?"

That's it. I grip the back of the chair she's in and roll her out of my way so I can clock out and leave.

A squeal leaves her and she claps her hands. "Was it good? It was, wasn't it? I mean, the man has feet the size of Georgia."

Whipping my head around, I gape at her in horror. Did she just reference Caleb's penis by his shoe size? Shaking my head, I exit the window and leave without saying a word. Her footsteps follow closely behind me, but I pay her no attention. Let the woman think what she wants.

"Want to grab some tacos on the way home?"

The mention of food sets off a rumbling in my stomach. I hit the elevator button and the doors open immediately. "Not tonight. Caleb is coming over for dinner." We pass the first floor then land on the ground level. I tap my foot as I impatiently wait for the doors to open.

"Oooh. McHottie is coming over for dinner? This is like a nightly routine with you two." I swear my friend is still a teenager at heart.

The smile falls from her face the instant the doors open, and her hand swings out in front of me, pushing me behind her.

"What the hell, Tracy?" That was beyond rude—she nearly took out my eye. Standing up on my tip toes, I see what alarms her. Blood, and lots of it. The hairs on my arms stand on end and my stomach turns. This isn't the first time I've seen blood; I work in a hospital, for Pete's sake. But unlike what I see inside the walls of the hospital, this is something else entirely. This is murder.

There is no other explanation for the massive amount of blood on the cement parking garage floor. It looks like a kiddie pool of blood has been dumped outside the elevator. I open my mouth to scream, but it freezes in the back of my throat.

Tracy pushes me further inside the steel box. "Stay put." She reaches over and jams her key into the lock, abandoning her badge and keys, then dashes out before the doors close.

My heart is racing. Whatever happened out there is not good, and my best friend just ran out into the middle of God knows what. Of all the things that could happen, why this? I want to remove her key and march out there with her, but I know that would be foolish. What I need to do is call 911.

It takes the dispatcher ten seconds to answer my call. That is ten seconds too long. Anything can happen in that short amount of time. For all I know, my best friend could be lying in a pool of her own blood by now.

Chapter Twenty-Two
Caleb

"What do you mean there was an attack near the hospital?" I slam my fist down on the kitchen table, splintering the wood. Alex had called to let me know that another body had been found. This time the body was found just down the street from the children's hospital where Desiree works. Thoughts of my girl lying in a pool of her own blood fill my head, and for the first time in centuries I'm sick to my stomach.

"Look, all I know is that Mac called after he inspected the victim, and said that we have another vampire killing on our hands." Alex exhales. "I know that your girl works at the hospital, and I hope she was nowhere near there when it happened."

His words are going in one ear and out the other without any recognition. My focus is on one person and one person alone. Desiree. More than anything I want her to be okay. I hang up, not caring if Alex had finished talking or not. I need to speak with her.

My heart is thundering in my ears and I can feel it pulsing in my neck. That pulsing is the weirdest feeling in the world, but is a testament to how scared I am for Desiree.

With shaky hands I dial Desiree's number. It goes straight to voicemail. "Are you kiddin' me?" I dial it again and I can feel the air thickening around me, threatening to choke the life out of me.

Again, the call goes to voicemail. I swear to God if a single hair on her head is missing, I will puncture this monster's skull with a pike and showcase it in my front yard as a warning to everyone that I am not a force to be reckoned with.

Third time's the charm, as they say. Wrong. Her voicemail picks up again, and my mind floods with images of my beautiful Desiree with rips and tears in her body and the Xavier emblem carved into her forehead. I let out a scream of frustration as panic settles in.

That's it. There is no way I can sit around, hoping she'll pick up her cell phone. I slip my shoes on without socks and race down the stairs.

"What's the rush?" Mike stands from a chair in the library, his eyebrows arching in concern.

I don't have time for explanations. My girl needs me, and unlike me, she's mortal and doesn't stand a chance of surviving an attack from an immortal SOB. "Alex called with news of another attack. I gotta get to Desiree," I call over my shoulder as I rush past him, shoving the door open with such force it rips from the hinges.

I can hear him calling for the others as I climb in the truck. The four of them have been with me since the passing of my father five hundred years ago. They are more than just my ranch hands, they are my friends and fellow soldiers for the vampire council. I trust them to do what needs to be done.

Leaving them to deal with the commands from the council, I crank the engine. Jerking the wheel hard, I hit the gas, peeling out of the driveway as fast as my truck will allow. There is no way I'm going to sit here and wait for news that Desiree is all right. I'll drive to that blasted hospital myself and find her. If anything were to happen to her, I'd lose my ever-lovin' mind.

I fumble with my cell phone while driving along this dirt path. Her number is still going straight to voicemail. Out of frustration I throw the phone back into the console and curse. Why is this happening? It's like the universe is trying to prevent me from any form of happiness. Screw that. I plan on having my happily-ever-after.

The sound of my ringtone sets my heart to racing. Is she okay? Is she hurt? Snatching the device from the console, I check the caller ID and grunt. Its Alex. Not the person I was hoping for, but maybe he has news about Desiree. "What is it?"

Chapter Twenty-Three
Desiree

Lifting my hand for the umpteenth time, I reach for Tracy's key but stop myself before my fingers touch it. Fear keeps me from turning her key and exiting this metal box. I glance at my cell phone, an act I've done nonstop since I have been locked in here. Still no service—I lost the signal right after giving the 911 dispatcher my location.

Sweat beads on my forehead and my vision is beginning to blur. Ugh, I hate elevators. I hate the boxed-in fear gripping my heart and squeezing the life out of me. Thoughts of suffocating in here all alone plague my overactive mind.

Pressing my ear to the door, I struggle to hear what is going on outside. No noise—I'm met with deafening silence. My breathing echoes off the metal walls surrounding me, taunting me with my lack of freedom. Thoughts of death have a vice-like grip on my heart.

In through the nose. I inhale deeply. *One, two, three, four, five. Out through the mouth.* Blowing out, I release a long breath full of tension. I repeat those words and actions over and over until my racing heart calms.

Images of Tracy beaten to death with a wrench swim in my mind, and I wonder what exactly is going on out there. Above all else, I wonder why she thought it would be a good idea for her to step foot into a dangerous situation. What good did she think she could do against a murderer?

If the fear I have for her is even just a fraction of what I will experience with my own kids, I'm not sure I want to have any. Worry is eating away at me. I wish I could get service in here just long enough to send a text to Caleb and let him know where I am. The last thing I want is for him to show up at my house and think that I'm standing him up.

The elevator doors shake from the force of being hit by an object — or possibly Tracy's body. Maniacal laughter sounds from the other side of those doors. The evil in that laugh causes the hairs on my arms to stand on end, and I back up to the far corner and crouch down.

There is no way that my best friend is going to live through this. Whoever is out there will kill her. She's a nurse, not a martial artist. I love her for trying to protect me, but she doesn't stand a chance.

Boom.

Air rushes from my lungs and my eyes bulge from their sockets. Was that a bomb? "What the hell is happening out there?" I shriek. I want out of this stupid steel box. Claustrophobia has already set in and my lungs are struggling to gain oxygen. I'm going to die in here, and no one will find me until it's too late.

The lack of oxygen sets my lungs on fire and my eyes water from the burn. I lift my phone to check the signal once again, but the tingling in my fingers due to lack of oxygen has left me with zero feeling in my digits. My device hits the steel floor with an echoing thud. "Caleb." My voice is a mere whisper.

Though I'm facing impending doom, my thoughts are still with Caleb. I hope he doesn't think I've abandoned him. This was not how tonight was supposed to go. We were supposed to

111

have a nice meal together and spend the evening cuddling on the couch, stealing kisses here and there. Maybe even taking Tracy's advice and having wild monkey sex.

Picking up my phone is impossible with my numb fingers — I'd have better luck picking up water. The more I try to grab the device the further away it slides. My last attempt to grab it sends it sliding across the floor. It bumps into the doors, tilting so the screen is facing me, and the screen lights up to reveal Caleb's smiling face.

Breathing is becoming a task too difficult to complete. An annoying ringing sensation is taking over my ears, and I can no longer hear anything other than the constant high-pitched whine deep within my ears. Hyperventilation sucks.

Dizziness causes my vision to wave like the ocean waters. Nausea roils my stomach and bile rises in the back of my throat, burning my esophagus. Blinking does nothing to clear the blur, and my eyes begin to cross. My heartrate slows dramatically as the high-pitched whine grows louder. I can feel myself slipping into unconsciousness, and the last thing I see before my world goes black is Caleb's face on my phone.

Chapter Twenty-Four
Caleb

I can smell the blood before I even turn into the parking garage. Holy hell, this murderous vampire has made his way to the children's hospital and attacked again. Panic sets in, and I have to fight the urge to abandon my truck in the middle of the street.

The first empty parking space available leaves me with very little room to get out of my vehicle, but I find my solution. Rolling down the window, I pull myself up through the opening and swing my legs out and over the windshield, walk over my hood, then hop down and sprint in the direction of the blood.

Desiree's friend, Tracy, is bent over and gasping for breath. Oh no, that's not a good sign. I pick up my pace, my eyes searching for my favorite girl, and then I spot something that makes my stomach turn. Body parts strung out in front of the elevator.

Oh God, I'm too late. That monster murdered the one woman that I believe is my soul mate. Anger rears its ugly head and red clouds my vision. My hands ball into fists and a growl rumbles out of my throat. I'm going to tear him limb from freakin' limb.

As I near Tracy, her spine straightens and she lifts her hands, palms up. Electricity sparks from her fingertips and pain radiates in my skull. *What the hell?* "Stop." My voice contorts from the

113

stabbing sensation above my right eye.

Her head whips around, eyes white and void of all humanity. I'm pretty sure that she intends to kill me, and whatever the hell she's doing to me is stripping me of all my vampire abilities. I swear to God that if she is the one who has been on a killing rampage I will send her straight to Purgatory.

My eyes move, briefly, to look at the blood. If she killed Desiree, I will have her head on a platter and serve it to the demons guarding Hell. Tracy blinks her eyes and the white disappears, her natural blue returning. The sparks cease and she lowers her hands. "Sorry."

Feeling slowly returns to my body, and the stabbing pain above my eye vanishes. "What on God's green earth are you, and where the hell is Desiree?"

"Desi," she shouts, and begins to bang on the elevator door.

"Tell me what is goin' on." My voice is harsh and holds a warning. The last thing I want is for my beautiful Desiree to be in danger from a woman that she considers a friend. Tracy ignores me and continues to bang on the metal doors in front of her. I grab her arm a little harder than necessary and spin her around to face me. "I demand answers. Now."

Her eyes narrow and her nostrils flare. If looks could kill, I'd be a dead man. This woman is on a mission, and she clearly thinks she's the one who deserves respect. Letting out a breath, she shakes her head in what looks like an attempt to clear the frustration. "Desiree is inside the elevator. I locked her in when I discovered the blood and sensed the vampire that was hiding in the shadows."

Shock from her use of the word vampire causes me to loosen my grip on her arm. I open my mouth to speak, but the words get stuck in my throat.

She jerks her arm from my grasp and places both hands on

her hips. "I'm a witch, moron."

A witch? I didn't see that coming. In all the years that I have roamed this earth I've only encountered one witch. That particular witch was responsible for the death of my father. Out of revenge, I tracked her down and ended her life. Glaring at Tracy, I point my finger at her. "If you've harmed one hair on—"

"Relax, she's fine." Turning her attention back to the elevator doors, she says, "Now use your strength and pry those doors open."

That command throws me off guard. How would she possibly know that I have strength? "What makes you think I can pry those open?" I ask, nodding my head toward the doors.

Arching a brow, she jams her finger into my chest. "I'm a witch, remember? I can sense your vampirism."

This revelation absolutely baffles me. How is it that she can sense what I am but I've failed to sense what she is? Taking a moment, I probe her mind. Nothing. That's impossible. I can read minds of human and supernatural alike. The tentacles of my mind reach out toward her again. Still nothing, just quiet.

"Stop trying to get inside my head, and use your bloomin' strength to get her out."

I guess I have a thing or two to learn about witches. Brushing past her, I grab hold of the doors and pry them open with little effort. This isn't how I imagined telling Desiree what I am, but there's nothing I can do about that now. Once she sees me prying these doors open with my bare hands, she'll know something is different about me.

The doors creak with the force of my strength. My eyes widen in horror when I see that the elevator is empty. I'm too late. That monster got to her before I could. How will I be able to go on living when a piece of my heart is missing?

Then I see her. Desiree is lying in the corner, unconscious. It takes exactly one second to rush to her side and lift her into my arms. "I've got you, beautiful. I ain't gonna let anything happen to you."

Chapter Twenty-Five
Desiree

Air whooshes into my lungs. I wheeze from the dry, burning ache in my organs. Pushing up on all fours, I continue sucking in oxygen, reviving my deprived lungs. Blood rushes through my veins and my heartbeat pounds in my ears. Taking one last gulp of air, I open my eyes.

Darkness surrounds me. Not even my hands are visible, and they're nearly touching my nose. In the distance I can hear Caleb calling my name. I open my mouth to answer, but the words won't come.

What is happening to me? The last thing I remember is standing in the elevator and Tracy rushing out into danger. Oh no. Tracy. A tear rolls down my cheek at the thought of losing my best friend.

Then my foggy brain registers the darkness and what it might entail. Am I still alive? Did that murderer kill Tracy and come for me? *Caleb.* My mind calls to him but my voice is failing me. I don't want to die and be eternally separated from the man that I'm quickly falling in love with.

Yet I fear that death has indeed come, and I'm now standing in the void awaiting my eternal fate. I'm far too young to die. Marriage and children were always high on my priority list. My life can't end before I've had the chance to enjoy the luxury of a family. A whimper exits my lips. *Life can be so cruel.*

"Desiree...." Caleb's voice sounds like it's a million miles away.

"She needs me." Is that Tracy? It sounds like my best friend, but her voice is just as far away as Caleb's.

Confusion overcomes me and I shake my head, not able to make sense of what is happening. The only thing I do know is that I need to get back to Caleb. Whatever is happening to me, I refuse to let it keep me bound in darkness.

Standing, I focus on the sounds surrounding me. Caleb and Tracy can still be heard in the background. Wind blows gently across my face, caressing me with life-giving breath. The sensations flowing through me are beyond anything in this world.

Warmth spreads throughout my limbs and electricity bubbles in my veins. Something is happening inside my body, and it absolutely terrifies me. Bright blue sparks flash before my eyes. As much as this experience is frightening, its oddly exciting. I can't explain why, but there is something about those sparks that calls to my innermost being.

My hands move of their own accord toward the sparks that are dancing before me. Part of me wants to pull away, but the part of me that's in control is reaching out to them. Caleb and Tracy's voices are nothing more than background noise, no longer drawing my attention.

At the near touch of my fingers, the sparks multiply and form a bright blue circle around me. I spin around slowly, looking for a way out. There isn't one. Blue flames border me and shoot up higher than my person, preventing me from seeing past them.

This is the most bizarre thing I have ever had the privilege of witnessing. I stretch out my arm again and the electricity gets brighter, dancing higher and higher. My heartrate is at an all-time high from both fear and excitement.

As my fingertips get closer, the sparks merge together and shoot upward for as far as I can see. The logical part of my brain tells me to pull my hand back, but I continue reaching out. *Almost there.* My innermost being longs for the contact, but so far, the flames have done nothing but distract me, preventing my touch.

Humming a soothing tune, I continue reaching out. Their dance becomes more frantic the closer I get. It's like we're both experiencing the same frightful and excited emotions. The blue flames long for me as much as I do them.

Then my fingers collide with their blue heat.

A surge of energy flows through my body, awakening every fiber of my being. I don't know what this is, but I crave more. Inhaling deeply, I press further into this massive blue spark of electricity. My hair lifts and my skin prickles. *Life.*

No, not just life. Magic.

I'm not sure what made me call this magic, but somewhere in the recesses of my mind I just know that this is a supernatural, magical thing—not a magical thing, but rather a magical being.

Chapter Twenty-Six
Caleb

It's been ten minutes and Desiree is still unconscious. I stand with her in my arms. "Something is wrong with her. I'm taking her inside, to the ER. She needs to see a doctor."

Tracy lifts her hand and I wince as she uses her magic to paralyze me, preventing me from getting Desiree the proper medical attention she so clearly needs. "She doesn't need a doctor." Lowering her hand, she gestures for me to sit. With her power, I have no choice but to obey.

Now I'm sitting on the cold, hard concrete holding Desiree in my arms and praying that she will regain consciousness. I don't understand Tracy's objection to Desiree seeing a doctor. As her friend, you'd think she would want Desiree getting the best possible care.

"Why isn't she waking up? Something is wrong with her. She needs a doctor." A growl vibrates from deep within my throat, and I can feel my eyes growing black from the power surging through my body.

"She's fine." Tracy glances over her shoulder at the police officers that are inspecting the crime scene. "Take her home, she's just transitioning."

I don't need to look in the mirror to know that my eyes are

about to bulge out of my head. This news takes me by surprise, and I'm left wondering if this vampire fed her his blood before Tracy ran him off. "What? She's turning into a vampire?"

Tracy surveys the area to make sure no one is in earshot. "No, dingdong." She points at Desiree. "She's a witch. Take her home and let her rest. She'll wake before nightfall."

The woman I'm smitten with is a witch? How the hell did this happen? After that witch killed my father I swore I would never befriend one. They were my sworn enemies. Now here I am falling madly in love with one. I can just see my father turning over in his grave.

Standing, I carry Desiree to my truck. Great. I forgot that there was a car blocking passage to the door, on either side. Thank heaven Alex chooses that moment to come zooming into the parking garage.

Tires screech as he makes a sudden stop in front of me. Jumping out of his car, he jogs to my side. "What happened?" Concern fills his eyes as they land on Desiree's limp form. His gaze travels back up to mine. "Was she hurt?"

"No." Unsure how to say this, I just spit it out. "Apparently, she's transitioning into a witch."

The look on his face says more than his words ever could. He knows how much I hate the witch breed…or how much I did. My feelings are beginning to change now that I know what my beautiful girl is. There's no way I could ever hate the woman in my arms.

"Look, I need to get her home, and those blasted cars are too close to my truck."

He peers over my shoulder to see what I speak of and shrugs. "Give me your keys."

I lift Desiree a little higher. "In my right pocket."

Alex steps forward and slides his hand into my pocket,

retrieving my keys. "Take the Maserati. I'll be there as soon as I've talked with Mac." Mac is one of us, a vampire, and he has been on the police force for years.

"Sounds like a plan."

I rush to the Maserati. Alex opens the passenger door for me and I set Desiree in the seat. Her head lolls to the side, so I recline her seat to keep her from hurting her neck.

As I squeeze into the driver's seat I'm reminded why I drive a truck. Small cars were not meant for tall guys like me. If I were human this would be where I would start to feel claustrophobic.

Alex waves as I back out of the parking garage, so I return the wave before pulling out into traffic.

The ride to the ranch seems to take forever, and I keep glancing over at Desiree to make sure she's okay. She seems to be fine. Her breathing is steady, and her heart is beating at sixty beats per minute. One of the many perks of being a vampire, enhanced hearing.

The instant the Maserati stops, Mike, Billy, David, and Joe exit the house and rush to the car. "Is she okay?" David asks.

"Yes." I heft her up into my arms. "I need to get her inside and lay her down so she can rest."

They step aside, making a path. As I ascend the porch steps they follow me inside. I rush up the stairs, taking them two at a time. Footfalls echo behind me. It's obvious they want to talk about the attacks, but they will have to wait until I get her situated. Desiree is my number one concern.

Marching to my room, I lay her on my bed. The guys are standing in the doorway, watching my every move but keeping silent. I grab a blanket from the closet and cover her body. "I'll just be in the other room, darlin'."

In truth, I have no idea if she can hear me. When it comes to witches and their transition, I'm as clueless as they come.

I'm hoping that she can hear me, or at least sense my presence. Leaning forward, I press my lips to hers in the gentlest of ways.

Witch or not, she is *my* Desiree. She holds my heart in her hands, and she is the one person that I want to spend my forever with.

Chapter Twenty-Seven
Desiree

Hushed voices penetrate my ears, disturbing the peaceful dream I'm having. It takes great effort, but I force my eyes open. The light filtering in from the other room pierces my eyes like a sharpened blade, and I grab my head with both hands, clamping my eyes shut.

Bile rises in the back of my throat and my head feels as though its splitting in two. Recent events come flooding back, and I remember what took place at the hospital. *Oh, God. I'm dying, aren't I? That murderous monster managed to get to me and tried to kill me.*

"Relax, Des." Tracy's voice is soft. Hearing her instantly settles my nerves.

I want to open my eyes to see her, to assure myself that she is indeed okay, but every time my eyelids slit open a stabbing pain pierces through to my skull.

"Don't try to open your eyes just yet. Here." She helps me to sit up and then places a warm cup into my hands. "Drink this, it'll help you to feel better."

I sniff it and immediately gag. This stuff smells awful. "What is it? It smells like crap."

The bed dips when she sits next to me. "Just drink it. Trust me." She guides the cup toward my mouth. "It'll help your headache."

My head does hurt. Maybe if I hold my breath I can get some of this nasty stuff down. It really does smell like dog crap. Taking a deep breath, I sip the warm liquid. As I swallow, it leaves a tingling sensation in its wake. I don't know what she put in this, but it definitely has a kick to it.

I inhale and the horrid taste lingering on my tongue hits me. The urge to vomit is strong, and I swallow repeatedly to keep the contents of my stomach down.

"Keep drinking," she urges.

Ugh. If this nasty crap doesn't cure my headache, I'm going to hit her over the head with a frying pan. To say that this tastes like a dirty butt would be an understatement.

"Come on, Des. You need this." She pushes on my hand, tilting the cup up against my lips.

I take a quick breath, holding it, and open my mouth in time to catch the warm liquid as it pours from the cup. Clamping my mouth shut, I moan around the liquid in disgust. Tracy slaps her hand over my mouth to keep me from spitting it out.

"Swallow," she demands.

I should be used to her nasty concoctions by now—she is always mixing up something to cure my ailments. Whatever she uses in them should really be banned by the FDA. My lungs begin to burn from lack of oxygen, and I can't hold my breath much longer. It's time to get this over with. Shrugging my shoulders up to my ears and tucking my chin to my chest, I finally swallow this god-awful stuff.

If my migraine doesn't kill me, this crap will. "Good." She takes the cup from my hands and I can hear it as she sets it on the nightstand. "Now, open your eyes."

What...does she think she's made a miracle tea that will

instantaneously heal me from this intense migraine? I love her and she's an amazing nurse, but as good as she is, she's not made of magic.

"Come on, Des. I need to take a look at your pupils to make sure you're okay." The bed lifts when she stands. "You were unconscious. You know as well as I do that you need to be examined."

She's right. I'd force her to open her eyes if the shoe was on the other foot. Taking a deep breath, I blink a few times then let my eyes fall open. Surprisingly, the stabbing pain is gone. Maybe my friend can work magic after all.

She pulls her penlight out of the front pocket on her scrubs and flashes it back and forth in my eyes. No wonder patients blink and pull back, away from the light. That little bit of light is blinding. She tucks the penlight back into her pocket, and I'm left with a yellow halo from its brightness. Thankfully, it only lasts for a minute.

"What happened?" I sit up and lean against the headboard. It's only now that I realize that I'm not at home. Not only is this not my bedroom, it isn't Tracy's either. "Where am I?"

"You lost consciousness for a little while, but I foresee a full recovery." A smirk lifts the corner of her mouth. "And you're at Caleb's." She wiggles her eyebrows. "In his bed."

I swear, my friend only has one channel in that brain of hers—the sex channel. Aside from her one-track mind, a smile begins to form on my face knowing that I'm in Caleb's bed. I have to bite the inside of my cheek to keep that smile from growing any wider.

"What happened back at the hospital? I was so worried about you when you ran out of the elevator and straight into what could have been a deadly situation." I'm so thankful that she is still alive. I don't know what I would do if anything had happened to her.

"About that." Tracy paces back and forth, not looking me in the eye. This is so unlike her. "I think we should talk about you and why you were unconscious, first."

Me? I would much rather hear about what she saw in the parking garage. "I'm fine. What I want to know is what you found out there."

"Trust me, it all ties together."

What is she talking about? How could my fainting have anything to do with a crazy lunatic out on a killing spree?

The look on my face must reflect my thoughts, because she pokes her head out the door. "Caleb?" She doesn't wait for a response. Instead, she stands at the foot of the bed crossing her arms over her chest.

Caleb must have been close by, because he comes waltzing in the room and is by my side within seconds. "Hey, darlin'. How ya feelin'?" He brushes a lock of hair behind my ear and kisses my forehead.

"I feel fine." His bright hazel eyes penetrate mine for a moment, then he takes my hand in his. "Have you seen the news? Do you know what happened at the hospital?"

The look that he and Tracy share gives me goosebumps. It must have been bad if they're not wanting to talk about it. His mouth is a tight line as he waits for Tracy to speak.

The silence is deafening. "Tracy?"

Her eyes meet mine and she lets out a breath. "Promise me that you won't freak out."

It's never a good idea to begin a sentence like that. This must be something major for her to act this way. "I won't freak out."

"Okay." She takes a seat on the opposite side of the bed and holds my other hand.

This is the most awkward thing ever. Tracy on my right,

holding my hand, and Caleb on my left, holding my other hand.

Tracy squeezes my hand. "You know how you've been experiencing headaches for the last couple of weeks?"

I don't want to talk about a few headaches that I've had. That's irrelevant to the conversation at hand. "Tracy," I warn.

"Look, I need you to understand that there are forces in this world." She bites her bottom lip. "Forces that may seem unbelievable."

Okay, this is getting downright ridiculous. "What forces? God? Yeah, I know that there's a higher being that exists in the universe."

She shakes her head, then nods. "Yes, but I mean that there are beings that walk the earth. Supernatural beings. They have been among us since the beginning of time."

Okay, my friend has fallen off her rocker. "What does this have to do with me."

Her eyes search mine, silently pleading with me to understand. "I need you to listen to what I have to say."

The suspense is killing me. "Just spit it out already."

Chapter Twenty-Eight
Caleb

I'm nearly bored to tears listening to Tracy fumble her way through this speech. It's clear that this woman has never had a charge before, and this is her first time explaining the paranormal. Watching a chrysalis while waiting for the butterfly to transform would be more interesting than this. By the look on Desiree's face, I'm not the only one who feels this way. I can't believe the witch council didn't train Tracy before giving her a charge. What the hell were they thinking?

I run my thumb over Desiree's knuckles. Tracy is doing a crap job of explaining things, so I'm just going to take over. "Tracy is trying to tell you that the paranormal exists."

Desiree lifts a brow. "Like ghosts?"

I smile. "I've never seen a ghost, so I don't know about them." Unlike Tracy, I'll just get straight to the point. "I mean, vampires, witches, and magic."

Her eyes widen for a moment, then she laughs. "Ha, ha. Very funny." She adjusts her position on my bed. "I love watching those types of movies, and when I have the time, I love reading those kinds of books." She chuckles. "But I don't believe in that kind of fiction."

This is a typical response from anyone who is being

introduced into this life. "Darlin', this isn't fiction."

Desiree eyes me curiously, unsure of whether I speak the truth or am pulling one over on her. "So, what, vampires stalk humans in dark alleys and burst into flames in the sunlight?"

"Not exactly." My woman needs physical evidence to believe anything that's being spoken, so I open my mouth and allow my fangs to descend.

Her eyes widen in shock and she gasps. "What in the world?"

All color drains from her face. Scooting away from me, she pulls her hand away from my grasp. It's evident that my fangs frighten her, so I don't try to stop her when she moves away from me. She needs a minute to digest all this information. I understand that. I've been there, it's a lot to take in. In answer to her question, I say, "I'm a vampire."

Before I can say another word, Desiree bolts out of bed. "That is impossible."

Tracy is quickly at her side, wrapping Desiree in a hug. "It does seem impossible, doesn't it?" Pulling back, she stares into Desiree's eyes. I really hope she can calm her down, I don't want to go chasing after the woman I love if she decides to bolt. Worry lines form on Tracy's forehead. "I'm your best friend, right?"

Desiree nods but says nothing. Her reaction is nothing I haven't dealt with before. I just hate having to deal with it with her.

"What Caleb has said, has shown you, is true. He is a vampire." I can see a light blue stream of power flowing from Tracy's hands into Desiree where she is still gripping her shoulders. I don't know the first thing about witches, but by the looks of it, Tracy is using her magic to calm Desiree's nerves.

"But that's not possible." Desiree's voice is much calmer now. Almost like she has been given a mild sedative. "That's make-believe. It's meant to entertain and nothing more."

Unsure of whether it's wise to approach her, I take a couple of steps toward them and stop with my hands up in surrender. "Darlin', fiction is based on pieces of reality. I am a vampire, and I'm as real as you are."

Her eyes move over Tracy's shoulder and meet mine. The fear that was there seconds ago is now gone. *Thank God.* "But how?" A thought occurs to her and she tries to back away, but Tracy has a good grip on her. "Are you going to kill me?"

It takes everything in me to not chuckle at her. What she has seen on television is nothing like reality. We are not killers by nature. We're not undead creatures. The undead would be zombies, and I have yet to encounter one of those since those things *are* fiction.

She has a lot to learn about this life.

The last thing I want to do is anger her, so I hold in my laughter and keep a straight face. "No, darlin', I'm not going to kill you."

Desiree's eyes are glassy now, which proves that Tracy did use her magic like a drug to calm her. "Aren't you supposed to be driven by a bloodlust or something?"

"Darlin', the things you're referring to is indeed fiction. Not everything you've seen on television is real. We're not driven to kill, and we don't burst into flames in the sun. Though we do need permission to enter a person's home." I can see that even with the calming magic, vampirism still scares the crap out of her.

"I can't believe that I've been falling for a soulless creature of the night." In her attempt to turn and run away, she stumbles and hits the floor with a hard thud.

My natural reaction is to run to her side and lift her in my arms. This, however, was a mistake. Desiree starts screaming and flailing her arms, which brings Mike, Billy, David, and Joe rushing into the room.

"Put me down." Those three words break my heart, something I haven't felt in centuries.

"What is going on in here?" David asks.

Desiree stumbles when I set her down, most likely from the magical sedative. "Your employer is an undead, soulless, human-eating monster."

Unlike me, David bursts into laughter, followed by Billy and Joe. Mike seems to be the only one of my friends that has any sense left. He crosses his arms and keeps his face blank. "Has he explained that he is none of those things?"

"Don't tell me that you buy his whole I-don't-eat-humans story." Desiree is struggling to keep upright. If she would just let me help her, I would carry her to a chair so she doesn't damage that beautiful body of hers.

"I do." Mike offers her a hand and she all too quickly accepts it, which is like a knife to my heart. Once he helps her to the bed, he says, "Has he done anything to you to make you believe that he eats humans?"

Hopefully he can get through to her. Having her this close yet so distant is killing me. I would rather die a thousand deaths than endure this kind of torture.

Those beautiful eyes of hers turn to me, and I hold my breath as I await her answer. "Well, no." She crosses her legs and leans back on her hands. "He's been the perfect gentleman."

Yes, it appears that Mike is beginning to break through that barrier of hers. "Then what would make you think that he goes around eating people?"

Tracy has now taken up the spot on the other side of Desiree, holding her hand. Oh, how I wish that was me holding her hand. I guess this is what they mean when they say love hurts.

Desiree stares at a spot on the floor. "He's a vampire." With a tear trailing down her cheek, she says, "That's what they do."

Chapter Twenty-Nine
Desiree

The tears won't stop. Crying in a room full of men is the most embarrassing thing I've ever done. *Please, God, let a hole form underneath me and swallow me whole.* Fiction is based on reality? There is no friggin' way. Yet, I've seen Caleb's fangs with my own two eyes.

"Why?" Mike's question draws my thoughts back to the present. "Because that's what you've seen on TV?"

I nod. "Well, yeah." On television those things are horrendous. Their natural instinct is to kill anything with a pulse. Even in my favorite television show, the good vampires still have a natural desire to hunt and kill.

The other guys, Billy, David, and Joe, all burst out laughing — again. Their lack of sensitivity is beginning to make me angry. Can't they see that I'm struggling with this? "Heartless dimwits," I mutter. My mutter causes them to laugh harder, holding their stomachs from the exertion.

My face is burning with a mixture of embarrassment and anger. If those guys laugh at me one more time, I will bolt from here. Even if that means trekking all the way home on foot. I won't stand by while they mock me.

Caleb clears his throat and the three of them leave the room.

That one small action does two things to me. It warms me that he cares enough to make them leave, but it also scares me. There is a dangerous look in his eyes, daring anyone to step out of line. I never want to have that look aimed at me.

"Look, vampires are not like what you see on TV." Mike shifts, crossing his foot over his knee. "I will admit that there are a small few that are killers, out there stalking their prey, but those would be the ones that were murderers before they were graced with immortality."

He makes it sound so normal to be a vampire, like they are no different than we are. No matter what he says though, vampires are not normal. They are immortal beings, and have fangs like a freaking animal.

Mike touches my arm and I look up at him. His face is devoid of all emotion, and I can't decipher his thoughts. "You are probably unaware of the number of vampires walking amongst you. Vampires have lived in harmony with humans for many centuries."

I seriously hope not. "What, do they hang out at the bars and night clubs?"

A smile lifts one side of his mouth. "No, though they enjoy those places the same as any human, they live amongst you. They are in the workplace; you may have even passed one or two walking through the park."

For one, no sane person is going to take a walk in the park at night. That's how you get mugged, raped, or killed. I open my mouth to say this, but he beats me to the punch.

"I know that humans do not frequent the park after sundown, but vampires don't just roam the earth at night." He slides off the bed and kneels in front of me. "We live normal lives...in the sun."

No amount of...wait...did he just say we, as in he is also a vampire? Ah, hell. What have I gotten myself into?

135

As if reading my thoughts, he opens his mouth and lets his fangs descend. I can't do this. Finding out that Caleb was a vampire was bad enough, now I find out there's two of them. Then it hits me. Billy, David, Joe. Are they all vampires?

Without a word, I pull my hand from Tracy's grasp and bolt from the room. I can hear Caleb calling my name, can hear his footfalls on the steps behind me, but I don't stop. I keep running.

The front door is within my sight, just five more stairs to go then I'll be in the entryway. Two more steps. One more. My feet hit the floor and I pick up my pace. I'm so close. Just as I reach for the handle, a large hand slams onto the wooden door, causing me to flinch.

"Desiree, please hear me out." Caleb's plea is strangled, like he is holding back a sob. His warm breath hits the back of my neck, and my body betrays me by leaning closer to him.

My heartrate quickens. He has never given me a reason to be frightened of him, but at this moment, everything I've seen is terrifying me. "Caleb, please, just let me go."

"Desiree, please." His voice cracks on the last word, and I almost turn around, but as soon as that longing hits me I remember the creature that he is.

I tug on the doorknob again and he lets his hand fall from the door. Throwing the door wide open, I run. My mind is on overload with all the vampire talk and I just want to get away, and I can't get away fast enough.

Dang, I left my cell phone inside. Oh, well. There's no way that I'm turning around. I'll just run until I get to the nearest convenience store, and then stop and call a cab. Crap. I can't even call a cab. My purse is inside as well.

This is not how I would prefer to get home, but I refuse to walk back into that house full of vampires. Worry for Tracy almost has me turning around, but she was in there talking about the paranormal like it was something she was used to.

Leaving her to her own devices, I continue my walk home —
on foot.

Chapter Thirty
Caleb

Watching Desiree walk — or run, rather — out the door, shatters what is left of my heart. Everything within me is screaming for me to chase her down and take her back up to my room and force her to listen to reason. The logical part of my brain speaks up and reminds me that she needs this time to come to terms on her own, so I do the only thing I can. I let her go.

She needs the space and time to digest everything she learned and saw today. This much I know. I just hope she listens to her heart and comes back to me. Living in this world without her is my worst nightmare. A world without her is a world I don't want to live in. I need her like I need the air I breathe.

Footfalls echo from the stairs behind me, but I don't care to turn around. In fact, I just want to go to my room and lay on my bed so I can smell Desiree's scent on my pillow. *I'm so pathetic.*

"Don't talk to me, you insensitive jerk." Anger is rolling off Tracy in massive waves, tainting the air around her.

"It's not my fault that you failed to tell her about our world," Billy seethes. Apparently, my friend thinks it's his place to remind Tracy of her failure. *Bad move, brother. A woman scorned and all that.*

A foot stomps, and I can only assume that it's Tracy's. "That may be, but you didn't have to laugh at her." Another stomp.

"She's out there upset, scared, and totally vulnerable." Air hisses through her teeth when she lets out a breath. "And she still has no clue that she's a witch."

I don't have the energy to deal with this right now. Turning around, I make my way toward the staircase, stopping in front of Tracy. "Find her and do your damn job. She needs to know what she is before she hurts someone."

Damnit, by all rights I should be the one out there searching for her, comforting her, and helping her with this change. She is my woman, after all.

Tracy's face is hard, either from frustration or worry. "I will." She lifts her hand, jamming her finger into my chest. "I like you. Don't mess this up with her."

She acts like I'm the one who forgot to teach Desiree about our world. *How about you focus on not messing this up with her*, I want to say, but refrain. "I don't plan on it." Leaving Tracy to see herself out, I ascend the stairs, two at a time, then round the top of the staircase and head to my bedroom.

Mike is still kneeling on the floor, lost in thought, when I step into the room. My footsteps spring him into action and he heads toward the door, placing a hand on my shoulder. "She'll come around. It's a lot to take in, and she just needs a little time to process it all."

Those words should comfort me, but right now they don't. I'm numb, totally and completely numb. "I know." The thing is, I know all of this. I've had to introduce my world to many over the years, and the massive knowledge overload is a lot to take in. People need time. I get it, I really do. But knowing it and experiencing it are two totally different things...and I hate this with a passion.

He looks like he's about to say something else, but pats my shoulder on his way out instead. On a normal day I would have asked him to go ahead and speak his mind. Today, however, I'm not in the mood. I want to be left alone to *pout*, as my mother would have said. Normally I would argue that this isn't pouting, but let's be honest…this is pouting.

The ringing of a cell phone startles me and I begin searching my pockets for my phone. Pulling it out of my back pocket, I see it's not my phone that is ringing. Whose phone, then? Oh, I hope it's not Desiree's. The last thing I want is for her to be out there, hiking back to her house, without a phone.

I fling the blankets back but don't see anything. Lifting the pillows reveals nothing as well. Then I see the light shining from across the room. Her phone is sitting on top of my dresser.

Slamming my fist on the wooden top of my dresser, I curse. What if Desiree needs that phone? On foot, it will take her a good twenty to thirty minutes to reach a store. I snatch up the cell phone and stuff it in my pocket.

I don't even make it halfway across the room when a shadow filters in the doorway. Looking up, I see Alex standing with his hip against the door jam, crossing his arms. The look on his face is serious, and that dread I felt a few weeks ago comes rushing back with the speed of a locomotive.

Deep inside, I know that the vampire Tracy ran off is not the only one causing chaos. There is another, possible several, that we need to hunt down. With that knowledge, I fear for Desiree's safety. Why did I allow her to walk out of my house without protection? At this moment, she doesn't know that she's a witch, and therefore has no idea how to use her powers. If these rogues link her to me and hunt her down, she will perish.

I tug my thumbs through my belt loops and rock back on my heels. "What is it, cousin?"

Alex opens his mouth, but stays silent for several beats. The suspense is killing me, and I snap my fingers to spur him into

140

motion. "I received a phone call after I left the hospital." He pauses, and an uneasiness churns my stomach. "The call was from Doris."

Doris? I cringe and raise my eyebrows with concern. I can feel the color draining from my face. A lump suddenly forms in my throat the size of a baseball, and I swallow, forcing it down. "That's not good. What did she want?"

Doris is one of the oldest vampires. She is also the head of the vampire council. Overseeing the safety of our race lies solely in her hands. Along with overseeing our safety comes the responsibility of deciding punishment for those who break our laws. If she is calling, then we are in bigger trouble than I originally thought. Now I'm really worried about Desiree's wellbeing.

Alex rakes a hand through his unruly hair. "What we know is that there are two rogues currently in Missouri, traveling in our direction."

Two rogues? That's not too bad. "Do we know what they're after?"

He pushes off the door jam. "Yep." His steely gaze meets mine. "You."

I can feel the change in my eyes and I know that they're as dark as midnight. "Me?" My cousin nods his head, stuffing his hands into his front pockets. Gripping Desiree's phone, I use it to send a text to Tracy. The woman has not stopped calling this phone since she left.

This is Caleb. She left her phone here. Find her, there's trouble coming.

I motion for Alex to follow me. With my nerves so high-strung, I need a bag or two of blood in my system so I can concentrate on the words coming from his mouth.

Tracy responds in seconds. *I'm on it. Thanks.*

I retrieve three bags of blood from the refrigerator, offering my cousin one and keeping the other two for myself. "Explain."

Hooking his foot around the leg of one of the barstools from the kitchen island, he drags it toward him then sits. "Do you remember Charles?" A glimmer of red dances in my cousin's irises. A sign that he is angry.

Taking a large pull from the blood bag, I suck it down with such force that the bag crumbles in on itself. "You mean the pathetic excuse of a vampire that sent that witch to kill my father?"

Alex nods. "Aside from those two rogues, Doris believes that Charles is coming to finish what he started so many centuries ago."

Rage like I haven't felt since the passing of my father rises within me. My hands tighten into fists. "So, he's escaped Purgatory?"

"Yes, and escaping the depths of that hellish place wasn't all he did." Alex gages my reaction, possibly trying to determine whether he should call the guys in for reinforcements.

He is right to gage and question my reactions. Rage is so strong in me right now, I may go postal. "What else?"

Bringing the bag of blood to his lips, he speaks before puncturing the plastic. "He freed Drake."

Drake is the second vampire to ever walk the earth, and one of the most powerful. Over the centuries his heart slowly darkened until he turned one hundred percent evil, craving the thrill that comes with the torture of humans.

Before being locked away in Purgatory, he tormented young women until their hearts couldn't endure anymore, then he'd rip into their carotid arteries with his sharp fangs and drain the remaining life out of them.

He is also the sire of Charles.

I fall onto the nearest barstool, slumping my shoulders and

flattening my hands on my thighs. Yes, I was the one that locked him in Purgatory, and I'd be the first one he came after. "Well, hell." Desiree's life is in more danger than I could have ever dreamed. "We need to find Desiree. Now."

Alex exhales, nodding. "I agree."

Chapter Thirty-One
Desiree

I don't know how far I have run. Not wanting to be followed, I took a detour through what looks like an apple, pear, and berry farm. Now, I'm wishing I had stayed on the main road. With the sun already setting it's getting cold out here, and I left my jacket back at Caleb's. "Smart move, Desiree, now you're going to freeze to death."

I hear footsteps in the distance and stop dead in my tracks. It isn't coming from behind me so I'm pretty sure that it isn't Caleb; but then again, I have no idea how fast the man can actually move. He is a vampire after all. If he is as fast as the vampires from *The Originals,* then he most certainly could be miles ahead of me by now, waiting to spring up on me.

Slowly I move behind the cover of a large tree. The sound of dead leaves crunching under my shoes makes me cringe. I hope that whoever is out there doesn't hear it. After what happened at the hospital, and then learning that Caleb and his workers are vampires, everything scares me.

I'm scared to death, and I just want to get home where I can feel safe again.

A twig snaps under my foot and I hold my breath. For several long, agonizing seconds I hear nothing. Fear has a tight grip on me, and I can feel my heartrate skyrocket. If I don't gain control of these emotions soon I'm going to pass out. Just the thought of passing out and being left vulnerable threatens to choke the life out me. *Jeez, when did I become such a baby?*

Out of habit I reach for my purse so I can call Tracy, but my hand touches nothing but air and then the fabric of my clothing. The reminder that I'm out here without a way to contact anyone forces a frown upon my face.

More leaves crunch. This time the sound is only a few feet away from me. If I move in the slightest I'll be seen by whoever is out there. My body stiffens and I press my back into the trunk of the tree, wanting desperately for it to conceal me.

Crunch. Crunch. Crunch.

Oh God, please help me. Now they're just an arm's length away. I'm going to die out here in the middle of this fruit farm, and no one will ever know. My body will rot away and be eaten by vultures, my bones buried by dogs, and no one will ever find me. Tears fill my eyes for fear of the unknown.

I'm almost positive that if my heart beats any faster I'll go into cardiac arrest. My face is starting to tingle from the lack of oxygen, and tears are steadily streaming down my cheeks. This is not how I want to die, out here in the middle of nowhere.

The sound of someone whistling in the distance draws my attention to the left. Leaves scatter next to me when a border collie takes off running toward the sound. *A border collie?* All the air I've been holding in whooshes out of me, and I bend over gasping for breath.

My heart is pounding so hard that my eardrums are vibrating with the pulse, I can't believe I'm this scared of the things unknown. It was a horrible idea to come traipsing through the unfamiliar farm at such a late hour. I should have stayed on the highway. Everything looks the same out here. Trees and more trees. My sense of direction is terrible, and I have no idea which way to go to get back toward the road that leads home.

Taking a chance, I head toward my left. Either I'll find a road or come across a house. Hopefully, I won't run into any killer vampires or murderers on the way. Oh, what a tangled web we weave. Can we just go back in time and restart the last several weeks? I just want my old life back. My normal life where, vampires are only fiction.

It's beginning to get dark, and I'm finding it hard to see out here amid all these trees. On top of that, I'm freezing. If I don't die by the hands of a killer vampire, then I'll likely die of hypothermia. Just my luck.

I'm not sure how long I've been walking, but it feels like an eternity. My teeth chatter when a gust of wind hits me. This would be the time in the movies when the girl gives up and lays in the forest, curling up into a ball, and is either killed by wolves or serial killers, or saved by her friends.

Well, I am not that girl so I keep trucking, picking up speed in hopes of warming up a bit.

Past the thicket of trees I can hear a car horn honk. I pump my fist in triumph. Relief floods me—I took the correct path and can hear the traffic on the road up ahead. Now, to find a store or café so I can warm up. This cold weather has liquid snot forming on the tip of my nose, which is just plain gross. I guess the good news is that it's not winter just yet. I'd hate to be a Desiree popsicle stuck out here in snow.

As I pass the clearing, I see it. Highway 177. I must be the luckiest girl in the world. On the other side of the highway is a small diner.

Chapter Thirty-Two
Caleb

Where is she? I have driven up and down the highway more times than I can count. Alex is in the Maserati traveling along all the side roads that lead toward town. Nothing. I mean, how far could she have gotten on foot? She's mortal, not a vampire with super-speed.

The contents in my stomach churn and bile rises in my throat. Something isn't right. I've had a bad feeling for a few days, and now that feeling is overwhelming me. Why does evil always seem to find me?

This time, though, it's not just me. Evil is rearing its ugly head, and now I've put Desiree right smack in the line of fire. Why is this happening to me now? Could evil not have come knocking last year when I was single and had no one to put in danger? No, of course not. Evil always waits until you have something, or someone, to lose.

My phone rings and the vibration causes the device to rattle against the console. I snatch it up and slide my finger across the screen to answer the call from Alex. "Tell me you found her."

"Negative."

A slew of curse words spews out of my mouth. "Where the

hell did she go?" A beep-beep-beep interrupts me. I pull the phone away from my ear to glance at the screen. Tracy. I don't remember giving her my number. "Hey, I'll call ya back. Tracy's calling."

"Okay."

A quick touch on the screen and my call switches to Tracy. "Hello."

"Please tell me that you found her, Caleb." Concern is thickening Tracy's voice. "I have searched everywhere. I even drove to her house in hopes that she called a taxi and made it home." She inhales and lets it out slowly. "Caleb, I'm worried."

Damn, I was hoping that Tracy was calling with good news. "I wish I had better news." My hopes of finding Desiree are slowly drifting away. If she would have never run into me at the club that night, then she would be safe and sound right now. Instead, she is out here alone and in danger.

I would love to think that because Drake is freshly out of Purgatory he's ignorant of my love for Desiree, but I know better. Being locked away in Purgatory doesn't mean being cut off from the comings and goings of earth. Purgatory has a wellspring where prisoners can go to stir the waters and spy on their loved ones...or their enemies.

In my gut I know he's the one that has been sending his minions out on attacking sprees in my town. Those bodies were left in places where he knew we would find them. If he knows where we frequent, then he damn sure knows who holds my heart.

"Do you have any witchy gifts that will help you track her down?" I'm desperate and am hoping for anything that will help me in my search for Desiree.

There's a long pause. "Yeah." She exhales loudly. "A locator spell."

I don't have a clue what a locator spell is, but if the name is any indication then it sounds promising. "Oh, thank God." The worry and anxiety that has been weighing me down suddenly lifts off my shoulders, and I relax knowing that we will find my girl soon.

"But," Tracy says, and just like that, the weight is back on my shoulders. "I tried a couple of times while I was at her house." A sniffle meets my ears and I know Tracy is crying. "I can't get a trace of her. It's like something is blocking me from reaching her."

Another string of curse words tumbles out of my mouth at this revelation. "How is this possible?"

"I'm not sure. She's just transitioning, so she doesn't have the power to block me." The sound of Tracy blowing her nose gives me the shivers. That sound is beyond gross.

If Desiree isn't blocking Tracy's attempts at locating her, what is? "What else can block you?"

"Another witch...or a powerful vampire."

A vampire? Icy tendrils wrap around me, squeezing me tightly. Fear taunts me, leaving me breathless. That fear rips my heart out of my chest and throws it at my feet, only to stomp on it.

It's Drake. I just know it is.

Tich Brewster & Shalisha Cooper

Chapter Thirty-Three
Desiree

The diner isn't very busy. Good, I would hate to come in during busy hours and not have the money to purchase something as simple as a cup of coffee. There is a small two-person booth in the far corner, and I head in that direction.

The hard seat is a welcome sensation to my overly tired body. After working all day with no time to sit down, and then the trek from Caleb's ranch, my feet hurt like they have been run through a meat grinder.

I want to slip my shoes off and massage my achy feet, but since I'm in a diner I think I will hold off. Doing that would show terrible manners, and I don't want to run off any remaining customers. Instead, I lean my head back against the wall and close my eyes with a smile as every muscle in my body cries out in blessed relief.

"What can I get ya to drink?"

I open my eyes and see an older woman standing next to me with her pen hovering over her notepad. "Actually, I just stopped to rest my feet for a minute. Is there any chance I can get a water and use the phone?"

Her eyes study me for a moment, searching. "Sure." She tucks her pen and notepad back into the pocket of her apron and

150

heads toward the counter, where she says something to her co-worker then disappears in a door off to the side.

The co-worker, an older man with salt and pepper hair, eyes me with what looks like sympathy. I wonder what she said to him to cause such a reaction. Moments later she comes back with a glass of ice water and a plate of eggs and bacon. The plate of food throws me off guard, and I look at the other two occupied tables, wondering if she's delivering food to one of them before she comes back with my water.

Nope. They have their food, so who is this plate for? A smile lights up her face as she places the plate in front of me. "I figured you were probably hungry." I open my mouth to object, but she talks over me. "No need in refusing this hot delicious meal." She sets a straw next to the glass of water. "It's on the house." Turning on her heel, she heads back to the counter to refill salt and pepper shakers.

As much as I want to refuse this meal and carry on about my way, I can't. I am starving something fierce. Today was one of those days at work. Two of my fellow nurses had called in sick, and one was a no call, no show. With the added patients to tend to, my lunch break consisted of a granola bar while I busted my butt measuring medication, answering questions, consoling parents, loving on kids, and filling out paperwork.

I shift in my seat so I can shovel food in my mouth without being seen by everyone. No one wants to see me eat like a starving cavewoman. The door chimes, and I'm too engrossed in my meal to turn around. Footsteps head my way, and for a split-second I worry that Caleb has managed to find me.

The dress shoes that come into view do not belong to Caleb, and I sigh in relief. I'm not quite ready to face him. The owner of the expensive dress shoes stops beside me, sliding into the booth to my right. I shovel the last of the food into my mouth then look

151

up.

The guy at the table next to mine is sitting so that his legs are stretched out on his bench seat, feet crossed at the ankles. His dirty-blond hair is spiked on the top of his head, and his icy-blue eyes are boring into mine. Nerves cause my abdominal muscles to quiver, and I quickly look away. I'm not sure why he stirs these nervous feelings in me, but I suddenly feel like his prey, and I'm already wanting to bolt out the door.

"I don't mean to stare. Please forgive me." He scoots forward and leans his forearms over his knees. "It's just that you look so familiar."

"Oh…that's okay." This is so awkward. I sip my ice water and smile at the waitress as she comes to take his order.

After collecting his order, the waitress turns around and clears the plate from my table. "How was your meal, sweetie?"

"It was wonderful, thank you." I feel horrible that I don't have my purse. This woman deserves a nice tip for her kind heart and excellent service. I'll have to make a point to stop by after I retrieve my purse from Caleb's so I can give her that tip.

She smiles, then disappears behind the counter.

The guy with the dirty-blond hair extends his hand. "My name is Drake. Drake Xavier."

I stare at his hand, still uneasy, but pushing that aside, I decide to be civil. Leaning over, I shake his hand. "I'm Desiree."

***

Drake is quite the odd fellow. At times he sounds like he's from another dimension. He uses terms that I've never heard of, and then brushes it aside when I ask him to explain. Aside from that, he's a nosey little booger, basically asking for my whole life story. Yeah, not happening.

Cutting a piece of his pie, he asks, "Tell me about your job."

"I'm a nurse." I'm not much of a talker, so my answer is short and to the point.

He smirks as if he knows all about my job, or that could just be my paranoia talking. He licks the crumbs from his lips before he speaks again. "What about your friends? Do you have any close friends?"

Okay, that's a bit personal for a stranger to be asking. I bite my lip as I look over at the exit. This is getting weird, and the desire to leave is so strong I can taste it.

He scoots to the end of his seat, leaning toward me. "Forgive me. It's just that I find you interesting. That's all."

"No, it's okay." Why did I just say that? It really isn't okay — he's kind of creeping me out. Those words are not mine, so why did I say them? "I'm a work-a-holic, and my only true friend is Tracy Harper. She works with me at the hospital." I don't know why those words fly out of my mouth. It's like I'm being controlled by an unseen force.

He smirks as if he knows all about why I'm just spewing out answers to his questions. "And what about a boyfriend? Is there someone special?"

"You know, that's really none of your...." My words are cut short. A warm sensation washes over me, and once again I find myself spilling my guts to this complete stranger. "His name is Caleb Shade. He owns a ranch not too far from here."

Luckily, I'm able to shut my mouth before I divulge too much information. Besides, even if I had told him about Caleb being a vampire, who would believe me? No one, that's who. People would think I'm crazy, and I'd end up in a mental institution.

Somewhere in the back of my mind, my internal warning bells are going off. Deep inside I know that Drake is dangerous, but I am not in control of my own body anymore. With every beat of my heart, another piece of me is slipping away. Soon, I'm nothing more than a puppet on a string.

Standing, Drake extends his hand. "Come."

My brain is cloudy, and it's getting harder to form a complete thought. I know that I should be frightened of this man, but for the life of me, I don't remember why. I'm not remembering much about him at all. Without hesitation, I place my hand in his and we exit the diner.

Chapter Thirty-Four
Caleb

I want to scream, to throw a major tantrum and break things. It's midnight. Desiree has been missing for almost four hours. Anything could have happened to her in that amount of time, and it would be all my fault because I let her walk out of my house. Instead of forcing her to listen to reason, I willingly let her walk out of my home, defenseless and vulnerable.

Since learning that Drake has escaped Purgatory, we have been out searching for Desiree. We have searched the highway, side roads, and the nearby orchard. I found a trace of her scent deep in the orchard. Once my nose caught whiff of it, I covered every square inch of that land, but found no other evidence of her.

Tracy is currently camping out at Desiree's house, hoping that she will eventually come home. She has called me several times in the last half hour in hopes that I have found Desiree. Sadly, I've had no such luck. I slam my hand on the steering wheel, I'm going out of my friggin' mind.

This dreadful feeling enveloping my soul and crushing my heart is unwelcome, and I'd like for it to evaporate. It doesn't though; it continues to wrap its tiny claws around my heart and squeeze the remaining life out of me. I can't help but feel like something terrible has happened to her. Surely she would have found a way to get in touch with Tracy by now. They are best friends, after all.

About twenty minutes ago, Alex thought it would be best if he went back to my house in the event Desiree decided to come looking for me. I spoke with him less than five minutes ago, but I can't stop myself from dialing his number again.

"No, Caleb. She hasn't stepped foot on the property."

My grip on the steering wheel tightens until my knuckles turn white. Not knowing whether she's alive or not is killing me. "Call me—"

Alex cuts me off. "You'll be the first person I call if she turns up."

Passing through a red light, I continue driving around her neighborhood, praying that I'll find her alive and well. The streets are dead, just the occasional car here and there. A chill runs down my spine and I break out in a cold sweat. Something is terribly wrong, I can feel it deep in my gut.

Movement in the bushes of a nearby house causes me to slow to a stop and scan the area. The glare from a streetlight is obscuring my view, so I roll the window down. I hear the crunch of dead leaves and I kill the headlights.

Seconds tick by, and they feel like hours. The need to find her and keep her safe is strong. Now I'm holding my breath so I can hear better. Movement rattles the edge of the bush and my hand reaches for the door handle, ready to bolt and drag her back into the safety of my arms.

A cat darts out of the bush and races across the street. Curse words that have no business being spoken spew from my mouth as I shift into drive. This is, without a doubt, the worst night of my life. Even the night I lost my father doesn't compare to the pain I'm suffering right now.

My truck has been on the road all night, I'm running low on gas and patience. The clock on the dash reads one fifty-nine. Any hope I had for finding her is slowly diminishing. Making a U-turn, I head toward Desiree's house. It doesn't take me but four minutes to pull into her driveway. The moment I kill the engine, I see movement through the curtain. Hope sparks in my heart, and I run like a madman toward the door.

The front door swings open before I make it to the porch, and my heart sinks when Tracy appears in the doorway. Her eyes are red and puffy. It's obvious that she's been crying. "I can't stand this. Something bad has happened to her. I just know it."

I don't say anything because she's right. Instead, I usher her to the couch and pull out my cell phone. This is much bigger than me, Alex, and the guys. It's time to call in some reinforcements.

Ring. Ring. "Caleb, what can I do for you?"

Good. Straight to business. I've always liked that about Ursula. "I need your assistance. How soon can you get to Shawnee, Oklahoma?"

"I can have Evan fire up the jet and be on my way." I hear movement on the other end of the line, then a knock on a door. "I need the jet ready to leave ASAP." Her voice is distant, like she pulled the phone away from her ear to speak. I assume she's talking to Evan. "Expect me in four hours, give or take," she says into the receiver.

I breathe a sigh of relief. "Thanks, Ursula."

"No problem."

I stuff my cell phone in my back pocket. Ursula has been my friend since the day I turned into a vampire. Like me, she works for the council. She is valued by the council because she has a very rare gift.

Ursula can see and smell a person's unique aura. It's hard for me to wrap my brain around it, as I don't have a clue what a person's aura looks like, let alone what it smells like. With this unique gift of hers, she is like a tracking hound. The council uses her to track down those hard to catch criminals.

What I'm hoping is that she will be able to smell Desiree's aura and help me find her before something tragic happens.

Chapter Thirty-Five
Desiree

My heart is pounding so hard it's echoing in my ears. Drake is a crazed lunatic. Earlier he was going on and on about betrayal and how he's going to torture his enemies. I look around at the room I'm in. There are no windows. The only source of light comes from a lantern sitting on the other side of the room. Black stains the concrete floor in several places. It's hard to see in the dark, but it looks like there's a car lift in the center of the room. This could have been a mechanic shop at one time.

It baffles me that I can't remember how I got here. The last thing I remember is sitting in the diner talking to Drake. That man is nosey, that much I do remember. Other than that, everything after meeting him is a giant blur.

I tug on the rope and wince when it bites into my skin. My arms are tied behind my back, and my feet are bound to the legs of the chair I'm sitting in. As scared as I was of Caleb, I wish he would come swooping in and rescue me, because I know that despite his vampirism, I'm safe with him.

Even though my wrists burn due to the friction from the rope, I continue to tug. I have to get out here. If I don't find a way to escape, I know I'll die a painful and horrific death. Wetness forms under the thickness of the rope, and know that I've drawn blood.

Laughter. Where did that come from? I thought I was in here alone. Has he been in here the whole time watching me attempt to escape?

"Yes, I have." More laughter. He's getting a kick out of watching me struggle. "You're quite the fascinating creature." He steps out of the shadows and slowly makes his way toward me. His dirty-blond hair is disheveled, most likely from running his hands through it.

My heartrate accelerates, and I'm once again left feeling like his prey. Since he was able to answer my unspoken question, I'm assuming he can read my mind. An evil smile gradually spreads wide on his face, and I know that I'm correct.

His nostrils flare when he inhales. Leaning closer, he inhales again. That's when his facial features contort. His eyes grow black, and a red ring encircles the blackness. There is something very animalistic about his appearance, and it frightens me more than I can imagine. There's no need for him to tell me what he is, I can tell just by looking at him. Thank God, neither Caleb nor his ranch hands had looked this way. What I see before me is demonic.

Drake opens his mouth and his fangs descend. "Your blood flows from your wrists." It takes everything within me not to scream. "I can smell your fear." His tongue traces over a fang. "Good. Fear makes the blood flow like a river."

If I wasn't afraid for my life, I'd make some smart-alecky remark. Instead, I close my eyes and pray that Caleb is ignoring my request to be left alone, and is out there searching for me.

My head is roughly pushed aside and his fangs pierce my neck, above my jugular. The pain radiates through my neck, and a burning sensation travels through my veins. Moisture forms on the surface of my skin as my temperature rises.

Breathing is becoming more and more difficult as he drains blood from my body. The intense pain scorching my insides mixing with the suffocation I'm experiencing is beyond tolerable. If Caleb doesn't find me soon, I pray death comes quickly.

Drake's shoulders shake with his laughter. The creep is enjoying my suffering. Oh, the things I would do to this monster if I had half the power of the hybrid — half wolf, half vampire — from my favorite vampire television show. Drake deserves an eternal punishment for his evil behavior.

A loud pop sounds when he pulls his mouth away from my neck. "You're an imaginative little twerp, aren't you?"

Pain shoots through my cheek when the palm of his hand connects with my face. My mouth opens and a scream erupts from my throat, both hurt and angry. His hand grips my jaw with crushing force, shoving my head to the side. Again his fangs sink deep into my neck, releasing toxins as he drinks.

Searing pain rips through my veins like molten lava, scorching every ounce of me from the inside out. Beads of sweat form on my forehead and upper lip, merging together and sliding down my face and neck.

Death is at the door knocking, begging me to let him in. His promises to ease my pain tempt me — I'm desperate to be free from this torment. This is not how I imagined dying. Car wreck, yes. Contracting a deadly disease from a patient, yes. Never in my wildest imagination did I think that I'd die at the hands of a vampire.

I hear a noise and open my eyes, but all I see is a blurry figure. My vision is failing me, along with my lungs. This person speaks, but I can't understand a word of it. It's like being underwater — everything is distorted audibly.

Drake's hand tightens on my jaw, and he releases his fangs with a pop before tossing me, and the chair I'm tied to, across the room like yesterday's garbage. I lift my head but I'm too weak; it falls to the concrete floor with a thud. The impact should hurt, but I feel nothing.

Screaming. Drake, or maybe it's the visitor, is screaming. Fear grips my heart with its wispy tendrils, wrapping itself around my tiny organ like a python. My heartrate drops quickly, too quickly, and darkness creeps into my vision.

My last thought is *Caleb, please find me.*

Chapter Thirty-Six
Caleb

Why does it feel like it's taking an eternity for Ursula to arrive? I glance at my watch, again. An act I've done repeatedly since hanging up with her. It's four in the morning. Ursula should be here any minute.

"For God's sake, sit down before you wear a hole in the floor." Tracy points to a chair across the room.

I had been so lost in my thoughts I didn't even know I was pacing. Offering her a smile, one that I'm sure looks as fake as it feels, I leave the room. Normally, I'm as patient as they come. Waiting has never been an issue for me. Then again, I've never been truly in love before.

Now, I'm wishing that I would have given in to my desires and had sex with Desiree the other day. Not to add another notch to my belt, and not for selfish reasons. I wish we'd had sex because I believe without a shadow of a doubt that she is my soul mate. When a vampire finds his soul mate, that soul-deep bond is not formed and sealed until the uniting of their bodies. Giving yourself to one another, heart and soul, tethers you together.

Had we had sex then magic would have melded our souls together, making us one. I would be able to feel her through our bond. I'd be able to speak to her telepathically from any distance.

163

Ultimately, that bond would allow me to find her. The unseen force that would bind our hearts, would draw me to her like a beacon.

Knock. Knock.

Following the knock is the sound of the wooden door creaking open. The noise springs me into action, and I rush back into the living room. Thank the heavens, Ursula is standing on the porch shaking my cousin's hand. She looks over as I enter the room, and offers me a genuine smile.

Tracy is on her feet, hands behind her back, and rocking on her heels. "Please, come in."

Ursula steps over the threshold, slowly, testing the boundaries. When she is met with no resistance, she rushes forward to shake my hand. "Caleb."

"Ursula."

Before I can utter another word, she turns her attention to Tracy. "I'm Ursula." She extends her hand to Desiree's friend. "I'm here to help find Desiree."

Tracy accepts the handshake. "I'm Tracy. Desiree is my best friend."

Ursula's brows furrow and she sniffs the air like a hound. "Ah, and you're a witch."

It wasn't a question, but Tracy nods anyway.

Ursula places her middle fingers on either side of Tracy's head and closes her eyes. The room is so quiet that one could hear a pin drop. Tension builds up in the air and wraps itself around my body. I'm tempted to take Ursula by the arm and bring her back to the task at hand, but I know better than to interrupt her when she is reading someone. Interrupting her would piss her off, and then she would snap my neck like a twig. I wouldn't die, of course, but it would paralyze me for a good forty minutes.

The loose change in my pocket jingles due to the nervous

bouncing of my foot. I jam my hand in said pocket and take to pacing the room once more. A hand lands on my shoulder, stopping my movements.

Alex squeezes my shoulder. "We'll find her." It's clear to see that he's saying this for my benefit, but his eyes tell a different story. Just like me, he believes that Drake has already made it into town, and has abducted Desiree.

I fear I'll never see her again. If that's the case, I'm not sure that I want to live on this earth any longer. "I hope you're right."

"Ah." The sound of Ursula's voice draws my attention back toward her and Tracy. "You've been assigned as Desiree's overseer."

I notice that Tracy has a nervous tick of her own; she's tapping her fingers on her thigh in quick jerky movements. "Yes." She rocks forward on her toes and lets out a breath. "She's in the transitioning phase."

Having already been inside of Tracy's mind and sifting through her thoughts, Ursula knows everything about Desiree and Tracy's relationship. Including the fact that Desiree is clueless of what she is. "And you haven't told her about your kind yet. She's out there alone and defenseless."

A tear slips down Tracy's cheek, and its only now that I see how deep their friendship runs. "I should have been a better overseer. If I had prepared her properly, then she would at least have an inkling of how to tap into her powers."

"Perhaps, but what-ifs will not help us now." Ursula turns her attention from Tracy to me. "I need something with her scent."

I nod and motion for her to follow me. As we walk down the hallway, I notice Alex pulling Tracy into a comforting embrace. Interesting. "I'm sure you'll find what you need in here." I push open Desiree's bedroom door.

165

It's odd watching her sniff Desiree's belongings like a dog. Yes, I've worked with her multiple times over the centuries, but now that its Desiree's personal belongings, it's the strangest thing in the world for me to watch. I want to snatch these items out of Ursula's hands and kick her out of the bedroom. Strange, I know, since I'm the one who called her here and led her to Desiree's room.

After smelling several articles of clothing and both pillows on the bed, Ursula stands before me with a frilly lace top dangling from her fingertip. "I think I've got her scent ingrained." Dropping the delicate material into my hand, she says, "Come on, lover boy."

As she steps out of the room, I tuck the fabric into my back pocket and join her in the living room. Alex is sitting on the arm of the couch, deep in conversation with Tracy. Her green eyes meet mine. The sadness that she harbored just minutes ago is now replaced with determination.

This girl is ready for war. Good. Now that Drake is no longer in Purgatory, that's exactly what we're facing. He's after my blood, and will hurt anyone with a connection to me.

Chapter Thirty-Seven
Desiree

Darkness surrounds me. Utter darkness. With the lingering effects of Drake's vampire venom, I instinctively reach up to feel the puncture wounds on my neck. Two sets of bites resembling snake bites mar my skin, and moisture rests in their cavities.

"Great," I mumble.

There is no source of light — I'm left with only pitch blackness. Lifting my foot, I discover I'm no longer bound to the chair. I'm free. Carefully I step forward, but stumble and lose my balance. My hands shoot out to break my fall, but I'm not falling. Gravity doesn't exist here, wherever here is, and I free-float.

This place is void of everything I relate to life — light, gravity, dirt. I should be scared, but I feel completely at peace. Unsure of how I know this, I know there is nothing to fear here on this plane of existence. I'm safer here than I am back in the real world.

In the recesses of my mind, I know this spiritual plane I'm in is safeguarded. No harm will befall me here. Whatever spiritual being is in this realm, it will protect me from any harm that may inflict my physical body on earth.

Stretching out my hand, I feel the space around me. There's nothing there, but the air is different here. It's thick, but the thickness doesn't suppress the oxygen. The only way I can think to describe the air in this realm is…alive. By saying the air is alive, I don't mean a living, breathing being, but rather life itself. Spreading out my fingers, I wave my hand slowly, caressing the air molecules. My hair lifts and a low hum vibrates in the breeze.

"You are correct, young one. I am life," a female voice speaks. Her voice is not from one specific destination, it comes from everywhere at once. The air twirls around my body, wrapping me in its warm embrace. "I am what sustains you. I am Silla."

"Silla?" When the name leaves my lips, the deepest parts of my body begin to warm. The warmth spreads throughout my limbs, mending the damage from Drake's venom.

I touch my neck again and the puncture wounds close under my fingertips. My lungs expand with newfound air, and the fog in my brain clears. Now I can recall every detail from my chance meeting with the evil vampire.

I remember him looking into my eyes, breaking my mental barriers, and compelling me to answer his questions truthfully. After he had gotten the answers he sought, he compelled me to go with him. I have never been compelled before, but it reminds me of *The Originals*. His compulsion was pretty much the same as the characters from the show, and my body moved of its own accord, obeying his every command.

Once he had me, he drove me to this abandoned building and bound me to a chair. Using his vampire abilities, he probed my mind and erased all my earlier memories. Rage fills my heart at the thought of a stranger invading my mind like that. Breathing deeply, I silently count to five, then release the breath.

The rage is still there, but it's not overwhelming like it was just seconds ago. I relax, closing my eyes and concentrating solely on the living air around me. Tingling sensations creep along my skin, giving me goosebumps.

I shiver at the blissful feeling flowing through me. Opening my eyes, I notice a soft bluish glow emanating from my hands. I look down to see tiny sparks resting on my fingertips, swaying back and forth.

"Yes." Waves of air blow my hair away from my face, lifting it to dance in the breeze. Warmth caresses me from the inside. "Draw from my power and allow me to fuel you." The wind picks up and the sparks on the tips of my fingers grow brighter. "Become one with me, Desiree."

This experience is one unlike any I've had the privilege of experiencing. Though I don't fully understand what's happening to me, I do have an inkling. Is it impossible for the air molecules to speak? Technically, yes.

Unlike air molecules, this is something much greater. This massive energy that is the air, is not just air. It's a spirit. I breathe it in and lift my hands in surrender, allowing it to overtake me, body, soul, and spirit.

The wind swirls around me. "That's right, my child. Accept me. Breathe me in, and I will give you power beyond your wildest imagination."

Yes, I can feel a strange surge of power in the air. It's calling to me, beckoning me to open myself fully. There's no doubt in my mind this power belongs to me. I can feel the familiarity of my ancestors in this wind. Closing my eyes, I open myself to this spirit of life.

Power surges through me. I can feel it racing through my veins, strengthening me. Empowering me. Every fiber of my being is awakening. My mind is eased of all pain and confusion.

As my soul drinks in this powerful energy, I'm left with the revelation of what I am. I'm a witch, but not just any witch.

I'm a Mortifera.

Chapter Thirty-Eight
Caleb

In the hopes of making this go quickly, I take Ursula back to my place. I'm standing next to Alex and Tracy as Ursula leans on my bed, sniffing the sheets and pillows. Like a blind woman with her hands stretching out in front of her, she waltzes out of my room and down the stairs, with us fast on her heels.

Taking her time descending the stairs, she sniffs the air, occasionally sticking her tongue out as if tasting the fragments floating in the air. My intestines are twisting into a bloomin' knot, waiting for her to get a move on. I understand she needs to take her time to properly track Desiree's scent, but heavens to Betsy, does it have to take this long?

Finally she makes her way to the porch, nose in the air, and continues to sniff. Seconds drag by like hours, and I have the urge to bite my nails. A habit I have never had, but the suspense is driving me up the friggin' wall.

There are a million images running through my mind on an ever-spinning reel. These images taunt me, showing me a hundred and one ways Desiree dies. Mauled to death, throat ripped out, heart torn from her chest cavity. Every scenario known to man is crossing my mind. The unknown scares me. Just the thought of her suffering because of my enemies makes me ill. Bile rises, burning my throat in its wake.

Ursula's shoes scrape the wooden steps of the porch as she takes them one at a time, sniffing as she goes. Alex and Tracy are at my side, the three of us following Ursula, trekking along the gravel driveway. Her head turns side-to-side as she sniffs.

I have a heightened sense of smell, but I wonder what it's like to see and smell a person's aura. For normal vampires, like myself, scent is something that fades over the course of hours. For Ursula, she can pick up a scent that is days, weeks, and evens months old.

Halfway down River Road, Ursula stops. Closing her eyes, she spins in a circle, sniffing as she does. "This way." She points toward the orchard. "She backtracked and went this way."

This much I knew; I went searching the area earlier in the day and had caught her scent. Part of me understands why she chose to travel through the farm rather than the road—she didn't want me to follow her. Though the protective part of me doesn't understand why she would willing put herself in danger just to keep her distance from me.

Thoughts of Drake torturing her fill my mind again. These images leave me uneasy, and anxious to locate her. Drake likes to torment his prey before going in for the kill. God forbid Charles has her. That man is as crazy as they come. The more I dwell on these things the angrier I become. Sadly, I can't get these thoughts out of my head. They are invading my brain like a disease.

With our enhanced speed, we travel at a faster pace than any human. Unfortunately, Tracy doesn't have this ability—but lucky for her, Alex has taken a liking to her and has been carrying her on his back.

I see that look in Alex's eye. My cousin may have found a woman that can hold his interest in something other than just sex. Of course, those two don't know each other. I've only witnessed him comforting her in this distressful time. Nevertheless, I hope he's found *the* one. I rather like Tracy, but only time will tell what their futures hold.

We stop and I take in my surroundings. This is the spot where I had detected Desiree's scent earlier. Ursula sniffs the tree where Desiree's scent had been the strongest. Turning left, she continues trekking through the orchard.

Weaving around trees, we finally come to the edge of the orchard. A paved road comes into view. Hope and dread fill me at once. Hope that I'll find her in some store or café, warming up. Dread that I'll never see her again or…I'll find her mutilated body hidden behind a dumpster.

Ursula sniffs to her right, pauses, then sniffs to her left. I worry my bottom lip as I wait for her to point us in the right direction.

When the silence becomes more than I can bear, she points to the diner across the road. "Her scent continues there."

I exhale a relieved breath at the thought of Desiree stopping at the diner. Clenching my heart, I smile and start to cross the road when Ursula sniffs the air again.

Her head turns to the left and she draws in a long breath. "Her scent goes across the street to that diner, but I'm picking up a faint scent, heading north. If I had to guess by the faintness of her scent, I'd say she hitched a ride."

All the tension that just left my body is now returning a hundredfold. That is the direction she would take to go home. Only she never made it home. All those images of her being tortured intensify, overcrowding my brain.

Alex squeezes my shoulder. "Cousin, stop tormenting yourself."

Right, my emotions are out of control, therefore my thoughts are a blaring siren to those around me. When a vampire is in an emotional state, their every thought invades other vampires in the vicinity. "Sorry," I mumble.

Alex places a hand on my shoulder. "We'll find her, and we'll kill everyone responsible for her disappearance."

Chapter Thirty-Nine
Desiree

The darkness of the old mechanic shop greets me as I open my eyes. No longer am I afraid. After I allowed Silla to merge with me, knowledge from my ancestors took root in my mind and soul. I'm a Mortifera witch. Mortifera are the strongest of all the witches. We are the only ones with the power to kill an immortal.

I'm not sure how, but the ropes that had bound me to the chair before are now lying on the ground in loose piles. I push myself up off the concrete. "Lucerna." As soon as the word leaves my lips, a fire burns in an old rusty bucket.

Along with the knowledge of who and what I am, I also have the revelation that Tracy is a witch as well. That discovery both excites and saddens me. It excites me that my best friend can share this life with me, but it saddens me that she didn't trust me enough to share this information with me herself.

This newfound knowledge grants me the understanding of what Caleb truly is. He's not the evil monster I once thought he was. Are there evil monsters out in the world? Absolutely. Evil monsters come in the form of humans, witches, and vampires alike, but evil does not take up much of the population. They're but just a small fraction.

A fraction that I plan to rid this world of.

Metal scrapes against metal. I back up a couple of steps, keeping my eye on the front sliding metal doors. One of them slides open with a hideous creak. Ugh. Somebody should oil those suckers. That's worse than nails on a chalkboard.

Black hiking boots cross the threshold with slow, calculated steps. The fire that's burning deep within my core burns hotter. You'd think that since the heat level within my body is so high, I'd be sweating up a storm. I'm not. It's like I am one with the fire.

Funny thing is, I've read books about supernatural beings, and this is how a few of them have described the witch feeling—this intense heat deep within their core. I always thought it was nonsense, just fiction written to entertain the audience. Now, I'm wondering if some of those books were written based on real life events.

Take me, for example. If someone would have told me that vampires and witches were real a week ago, I would have laughed at them until my face was blue. Now that I'm living it, I have a whole new perspective on the supernatural world.

A maniacal laugh pierces the air. Just the sound of that laughter stirs the fire within me. "Lucerna." A metal trash bin catches on fire, illuminating the area and giving me a good glimpse of the intruder.

His cotton-white hair is unkempt and frizzy on the top of his head. Blood red eyes are staring at me hungrily. "What do we have here?" The speed at which he moves is unlike anything I've ever seen. He is crossing the shop space in less than a second. "I hate witches. Your kind are nasty little vermin."

Spit flies out of his mouth when he speaks, leaving slimy droplets on my face. I wipe the wetness from my cheek and the corner of my mouth. *Disgusting.* He circles me, eyeing me from head to toe. A growl escapes his lips and he shoves my shoulder, causing me to stumble.

"You had no power a few hours ago, when we left you." His dirty hand grips my face, jerking my head so our eyes meet. "That means that you're a newbie, with no clue how to properly use your powers." The smile that spreads on his face is full of malice.

He thinks I'm clueless. Funny. I'll let him believe that, for now. My guess is he's working with Drake. Maybe he works for Drake. Either way, it doesn't matter. What matters is that I plan on killing these fools and getting the hell out of here. To do that, I need to play dumb so I can figure out who all is involved.

"You're right." I cast my eyes downward, feigning cowardice. "I was never taught the things of this supernatural world. Heck, I didn't even know about vampires and witches until a few hours ago."

A smile of pure wickedness forms on his face, and his fangs protrude from the corners of his mouth. "Music to my ears. Your fear will season your blood." His tongue darts out, sliding across his lower lip. "I can't wait to taste you."

"Born to Be Wild" blasts from his back pocket and he reaches for his cell phone. Tapping the screen, he grunts, "Yeah?"

The *tap, tap, tap* of his hiking boot on the concrete as he taps his foot is enough to drive a person insane. It also gives away his anxiety. Who is on the other line, and what has this man so anxious? He says nothing, just listens to the caller. I wish I had super hearing like the vampires on television.

His head jerks in my direction, and his red eyes darken to the color of a raven, with flecks of red shining in their depths. The change startles me, making my skin crawl. "Yes." Ending the call, he stuffs the cell phone back into his pocket.

I wonder what that was all about. Whatever it was, it definitely darkened his mood.

The chain jingles in his hand when he steps closer to me. I had been so focused on playing dumb that I didn't even see the chain. "Wish I could stay and chat." Gripping my wrists in one hand, he wraps the chain painfully around my hands, securing it to a hook on the lift behind me. "But duty calls."

Placing a nasty, sloppy kiss to my jugular, he's out the door before I can utter a word. Great, now I'm slung up like a slab of meat.

Chapter Forty
Caleb

The morning sun is beginning to rise. We have traveled miles past Desiree's neighborhood. Given the fact that we're still on Highway 177, I'm starting to think that Ursula has lost track of Desiree's scent.

A knot twists and forms in my stomach, and nausea sets in. Nausea. I haven't been nauseous since before I became a vampire. I have to say, I hope to never feel this way again. It sucks. How on this green earth do pregnant women deal with morning sickness on a daily basis? I can hardly handle this little bit of nausea. Ugh. Thanks, but no thanks.

Ursula's movements cease. The beating of my heart increases, thinking that she's finally found Desiree. I look around us, but all I see is the highway and overpasses. Not a single building is in sight. Then she spins on her heel. "How long have we been friends?" she asks me.

I'm a little thrown off by her question. "Roughly six hundred years."

The hardness that was in her gaze just moments ago starts to vanish. The edge I once saw is now softening. "Right. Can you tell me why we don't bring soldiers who have a personal connection to the victim with us into battle?"

I get it now. In my heightened state, I'm broadcasting to every vampire within a two-mile radius. "Because they jeopardize the mission." What she brings up is valid. Not only am I broadcasting loud and clear who we're looking for, I'm also giving away our location.

Jamming her finger into my chest, she says, "Great. Now get control of yourself or go home. Am I understood, soldier?"

"Yes, ma'am." It's been five hundred years since anyone has given me orders, and it stings just a little. Squaring my shoulders, I buck up and act like the soldier that I am, cowboy boots and all.

A chuckle meets my ears, and their tips burn from the anger and embarrassment flowing through me. Embarrassment because my scolding took place in front of Desiree's best friend. Anger because Alex is laughing at me.

A pair of black chucks with skull imprints step into view. I glance up at Alex, who is wearing an amused grin. He's slightly leaning forward from the weight of Tracy on his back. Her legs dangle through the hook of his arms, and her head is resting on the top of his head. The shine in her eyes is testament to the fact that she is also enjoying my little scolding. Great. Just great.

"Dang, cousin, you just got burned."

Thank you, my dear cousin, for adding to my embarrassment. "Shut it, Alex."

The longer we stand here chatting the longer Desiree remains in danger. I'm ready to rescue my sweet damsel in distress and go home. Whether she wants to go back to her place or is willing to join me at the ranch, I don't plan on leaving her side. Ever. Her demands for space be damned.

Ursula's face is void of any emotion. This is what makes her good at her job, she completely detaches from all emotion, just flips it off like a switch. Without a word, she continues trekking down the highway.

179

Minutes pass. For us that means we've traveled another several miles at our inhuman speed. Ursula stops to sniff the air then veers to the right, taking Highway 66. We pass cars right and left, the drivers unaware of our presence since our speed is too swift for their human eyes.

Now that my mind is clear of my emotional state, my focus is sharp. I can now function with clarity, as a great vampire soldier should.

Ursula comes to a screeching halt. With my eyes and ears focusing on our surroundings, I don't notice her still form until I nearly collide with her. Thank God for quick reactions. I swerve just in time to prevent the collision, saving myself from a horribly embarrassing tumble.

Looking toward the exit and back ahead, Ursula sniffs and squints at the air simultaneously. "Her scent goes that way." She points to the exit on the left. "But the scent of the one she travels with continues up ahead."

I can't believe that I haven't thought to ask her this before. "Do you recognize the scent of her travel companion?" Inhaling deeply, I prepare for the name I know she's going to say.

"Yes." She looks to her left, then to the right. Tilting her head in the direction of the exit, she speeds across the highway.

I'm close on her heels. When she comes to a stop at the end of the exit, I ask, "And who is she traveling with?"

Ursula doesn't say a word, but her eyes are filled with pity. That look tells me all I need to know. Drake is responsible, and this time I will have his head on a stick. Killing him is not something I can do on my own, I'll need a Mortifera witch. Lucky for me, I know a witch that can help me find one. Tracy.

"Right now, we need to focus on Desiree. Just the mention of her travel companion and you've turned your emotions back on. Shut that switch off and leave it there until the mission is over."

Ursula points north. "Her scent continues up this road."

I glance ahead. Road 3370 looks like it leads to a small hick town. Good God, I hope her scent ends somewhere in this town. I don't think I can go another thirty miles without losing my damn mind.

We're traveling at a high speed, the town whipping by in a blur. The road continues for another mile and dead ends at an empty pasture. Well, mostly empty. There is an old rusty mechanic shop in the middle of the land.

What starts my heart to pumping is the fact that the old abandoned building is on fire. I grip Ursula's arm a little tighter than I mean to. "Tell me her scent goes beyond that building."

The muscles in Ursula's arm tense and she pulls away from my hold. I fully expect for her to scold me for strong-arming her, but the lecture never comes. In fact, she is refusing to look me in the eye.

Sweat beads on my forehead and the blood I consumed earlier threatens to make a reappearance. "Damnit, Ursula, tell me that Desiree's scent does not end at that burning building."

"I'm sorry."

Cries fill the air behind me and I can hear Alex shushing Tracy. As much as I'd like to turn around and offer a few words of comfort to Tracy, I can't. I can't even turn around to look at her, because the moment I do, I know that I'll lose what little strength I have left.

Rather than listening to apologies and sympathies, I swallow the large lump in my throat and march forward. I have to see her for myself. What kind of man would I be if I didn't inspect with my own eyes?

Voices. I hear them speaking, whether it's to me or just amongst themselves, I don't know. Every sound around me is nothing more than an annoying buzz. I feel hands gripping me, pulling me back, but I shrug them off and continue my trek toward the blazing fire.

Chapter Forty-One
Desiree

I guess that cotton-haired freak thinks these chains will keep me captive. If only he knew. A laugh rumbles out of my chest. Drake and this fool of his have sorely underestimated me. Hell, if I hadn't had that strange encounter with Silla, the bringer of life, then I would be underestimating myself.

The moment I opened myself to her and allowed her to become one with me, I grew in knowledge. Knowledge like I've never known before. Now that I have her essence flowing through my veins, I have all the knowledge and power of every one of my ancestors.

Talk about weird. This tops my list. "Retexere." Unravel.

The chains binding my wrists begin to loosen. My feet are barely touching the floor, so I have no way of lifting my body enough to remove the chain from the hook above me. Wriggling my hands, I try working the loops wider so I can free myself.

"Retexere." The chains loosen more. It's just enough to give me hope, but not enough to actually break free. Taking a deep breath, I close my eyes.

"Libera me." Free me.

The chains screech and pop as the links break, one by one. *Pop, clang. Pop, clang. Pop, clang.* The chain links continue to break

183

until my feet are flat on the ground and my hands are free. *Perfect.* A smile stretches across my face. That burning flame in my soul rises, and powers of old race through my bloodstream. The heat is on; I've got power, and I'm killing a monster as soon as I open these doors. Those vile beasts have started a war, and I intend to end it.

Rubbing the redness on my wrists, I curse. That maggot had me tied so tightly that the top layer of epidermis has broken in several places. My breathing escalates and my pulse quickens. Anger boils just under the surface, waiting to be let loose. In due time. I'm saving that angry power for the fools who've been holding me captive.

With slow, even steps, I make my way to the double doors. Unsure how many people this vampire has working for him, I press my ear to the door. I don't hear anything. Erie silence meets my ears, making me cringe.

The calm before the storm.

I push on the doors to no avail. On the other side of the door, a heavy chain rattles against the metal handle. Of course, they threaded a chain through the door handles to lock me in.

A giggle rises, bubbling up my throat. The sound is a mixture of anger, amusement, and revenge. *Did that come from me?* I know it did, but it surprises me that a sound so vicious could come from my lips. Like a drug, the giggle fuels my drive to tap into my powers.

"Erumpere." Break free. The words come forth with authority.

The air in the building swirls around me, lifting my hair within its funnel. The doors rattle. Their movement increases the tension I feel in my belly. Lifting my hands, palms up, I focus on breaking free from this prison.

"Erumpere." The rattling of the doors increases, the screech of metal on metal piercing my ears. "Nunc," I shout.

Thunder booms outside and the doors burst from their hinges, shattering as they fly through the air like ninja stars. The sharp pieces of metal embed in a nearby tree. *Wow. That's the most amazing thing I've ever seen.* Power like that, I thought, was only written for television, but here I stand, staring at the evidence of my power.

Footsteps echo from the clearing in the trees, off to my left. The stench of decay wafts in the air. Instinctually, I know this smell is coming from the type of vampire that Caleb tried to tell me about. One who has given in to the evil that hell has to offer.

This odor is stronger than the one that came from the cotton-haired vampire. Does that mean his heart is tainted more than the other vampire? Or, possibly that my sense of supernatural scent hadn't quite developed when the other vampire was in my presence? Who knows. All I know now is that this vampire is evil, and he is after me.

The footfalls grow louder the closer he, or she, gets. I widen my stance, lift my hands, and call to the elements of the earth to aid me. Tree branches sway with the force of the wind, and dead leaves blow in swirling patterns along the ground.

Whoever is coming, they're almost here.

Movement in the trees beyond catches my eye, but it's too fast for my eyes to focus on. For the first time in my life I'm in a dangerous situation, and I'm not fearing for my life. Taking a deep breath, I allow the scent of the earth to merge with my powers.

Movement so fast that its nothing more than a blur races toward me.

Bam. The vampire clashes with the wall of air that's surrounding me. He brushes his fiery-red hair out of his eyes. A brow raises high on his head. Confusion. He lifts his hand and slowly reaches out to me. Midway, his hand slams into an invisible wall, and he growls in frustration.

Menacing eyes glare at me. "I hate witches."

"I'm not so fond of you either."

His bare feet leave imprints in the dirt as he walks a slow circle around me, testing my magical barricade. I turn with his movements, never letting him out of my line of sight. Red blazes in his irises. He's furious. Well, so am I. How dare these idiots kidnap me and hold me hostage?

A growl rumbles out of his throat and he lunges forward. The invisible shield holds strong, sparking on impact and singeing the hairs on his arms. Baring his fangs, he lunges again. I smile smugly. His vampire power is nothing compared to mine.

"You stupid brat." Spittle flies from his lips when he speaks. "I'm going to kill you and enjoy every last drop of your blood."

His words roll right off my shoulders. They mean nothing to me. "There's a better chance of hell freezing over."

"You talk mighty big for a newly transformed witch." Amusement sparkles in his eyes. "By the way, how is Caleb?"

His question throws me off guard and my shield wavers for a brief second. It's just the opportunity that he's hoping for. Lunging forward, he grabs hold of my throat, crushing my trachea. *Pop.* The sound of my windpipe bursting startles me. Tears run down my cheeks from the burn in my throat.

"Ah, so you truly are his puppet?" The word puppet falls from his lips like venom. "Oh, sweet revenge."

Revenge? Revenge for what? The grip on my throat tightens. Pressure builds up behind my eyeballs and spots of light float in my vision.

"Caleb should have known better than to fall in love with a mortal." A laugh erupts from his chest. "Don't worry, I won't kill you, *yet*."

I blink, trying to bring my eyes into focus.

186

"I want him to watch as I end your miserable life. I'm going to enjoy his pain and grief when he watches your life essence escape your body." He must see the question in my expression. "A life for a life. He sentenced my mother to a life in Purgatory, and for that he must pay."

Blackness threatens to overtake me. I'm not sure how much longer I can hold on. *Focus on my energy flowing through your veins,* Silla's voice whispers in my mind.

I'm not sure how I'm going to focus when I'm on the verge of passing out from lack of oxygen. Despite the burn in my lungs, the pain in my throat, and the pressure behind my eyes, I focus on Silla.

I remember being in her presence and the absolute calm that I felt. Allowing her essence to fuel my soul, empowering me. Hunger courses through me. Hunger for her and the power she offers.

Every molecule in my body opens to her. Her essence feeds me. Supernatural oxygen fills my lungs, easing the burn. My trachea restructures beneath the hands of my enemy, allowing me to breathe. Blood rushes into my tissues, feeding and strengthening my muscles.

The red-haired vampire's eyes widen in shock. "What the hell?" Heat courses through me. Energy builds in my core. His hands fall from my neck, eyes unblinking as he stares at me. "This cannot be."

He takes a measured step back. The wind picks up around us, forming a tornado of sorts. Fear flashes in his eyes, his Adams apple bobbing when he swallows. I don't need a mirror to know that my eyes are different. I can feel their change, though I have no idea what they actually look like.

Power is radiating off me and the vampire takes another step back. When his back hits the wall of the tornado it throws him at my feet. The terror in his eyes fuels the tornado, and the winds pick up speed.

Pointing a finger at him, I say, "Adolebit."

All color drains from his face. He opens his mouth, but before he can get a word out, he bursts into flames. The tornado lifts his burning body into its cyclone, the flames becoming one with the wind and turning into a massive tornado of fire that carries his burning body into the old mechanic shop.

The whirlwind of fire is so massive that it engulfs the building where I was held captive. *Good riddance.*

My body is weak—I'm losing every ounce of strength I have. When the metal of the building screams under the fierceness of the fire, my knees buckle and I land on the ground, watching the building burn.

Chapter Forty-Two
Caleb

Rocks crunch under my feet as I race toward the burning building. My stomach twists in knots, knowing that Desiree could be trapped inside. God, I hope she's not in there. If she was, I pray she either found a way to escape or that Ursula has miscalculated Desiree's scent.

In truth, Ursula never miscalculates. She has never been wrong when tracking a supernatural being. Sweat trickles down my neck, soaking into the collar of my shirt. The moment that my feet hit the dry grass, I come to a screeching halt, unsure if I want to continue. What if I rush in and discover her body is burned to a crisp? I wouldn't be able to handle that.

Dead leaves crunch behind me and a set of black chucks decorated with skulls stop beside me. Alex squeezes my shoulder. "You can do this, cousin. I'm right here."

Alex and I may be total opposites, and we fight regularly, but I know beyond a shadow of a doubt that he has my back. Always has and always will. He will be here for me, and do whatever it takes to find those responsible for Desiree's death.

"So am I." Tracy's voice startles me.

I've been focusing on the task and worrying so much about how Desiree may have been tortured to death that I've forgotten

189

Tracy is with us. As to not be rude, I glance up at her, where she's still clinging to Alex's back, and I smile.

Together we march toward the building. My stomach contracts with every step I take. Finding your soul mate is a once in a lifetime thing. I'm not sure I want to live the rest of my existence without her. I refuse to mention this to Alex, but as soon as Drake and every last one of his disciples are dead, I plan on begging the Mortifera witch we hire to execute them to grant me the same fate.

The heat from the fire is intense. Flames lick the air, gaining energy from the oxygen. Sweat is pouring off me, soaking my clothes. Smoke fills my nostrils, causing me to cough and gag.

There's no way I can enter that building. I may be an immortal, but the flames will burn the flesh from my bones, preventing me from taking more than two steps inside. Then it'll take several days and many gallons of blood to repair the damage it will cause.

"Step back, boys." At Tracy's command, Alex sets her on her feet and takes me by the arm, pulling me back. I watch as Tracy lifts her hands in the air — the winds calm and blow gentle caresses through her hair. Aiming a finger at the burning building, she says, "Cessaverunt."

The flames cease licking the air, descending into the building. The whirlwind that was once a tornado of flames is now an orange glow that's visible through the open doors. I rush forward, ready to dart inside, when I hear it. Labored breathing.

The need to dash inside and find Desiree's remains is strong, but I can't ignore the fact that someone is nearby. It could be an innocent human for all I know. Turning around, I bring my finger up to my lips to signal the others to remain quiet. Alex lifts an eyebrow in question, so I point to my ear then to the left, conveying for him to listen to the sounds in that direction.

He tilts his head, then raises an eyebrow. The four of us round the side of the building, fully preparing for any threat that may be waiting for us. My eyes search the landscape, but I don't see anyone. Other than the smoky building, there is nothing out here but a stack of melting tires that are stacked next to the old shop.

Relaxing my tense shoulders, I clear my head and listen again. There it is. The heavy breathing is up ahead. I take a step forward and a gust of wind blows against me, pushing me back. *What in the world was that?*

Glancing at Tracy, I raise my brow. Her expression is one of shock.

Ursula points in the direction the breathing is coming from. "Those colors. They're hers, but they're different. Before, she had a beautiful mixture of purples, pinks, and blues. Now there's a mix of greens, yellows, and reds added to the other colors."

Every word coming from Ursula's mouth is a foreign language to me. Telling me about Desiree's colors is like speaking Greek to the residents of Oklahoma. Unless they study that language, they have no clue what you're talking about. Same goes for me and Ursula's gift. It's all Greek to me. "You know, I have no clue what that even means."

Tracy lifts her hands, palms out. The posture looks like she's pushing against the wind with her hands, which I know is physically impossible. I watch in amazement as the wind slows, then settles. Must be her magic at work. Nice.

Just as quickly as it subsides, the wind builds up, then shoves us all backward. Damn, dirt is blowing into my eyes. I blink rapidly, trying to remove the small pesky particles.

Tracy stomps her foot and shoves against the wind. It takes longer for the gusts to slow, but once they die down, I rush forward. "Desiree?"

All at once the wind dies and leaves fall to the ground at my feet. "Caleb?"

I let out a sigh of relief. "Thank God." I'm at her side within seconds. Desiree is laying on her side, legs curled close to her body. Kneeling, I scoop her up into my arms and cradle her against my chest. "I'm right here, darlin'."

Her arms wrap around my neck and her tired eyes gaze into mine. "I'm glad you're here." A yawn escapes her. "I'm so tired."

"That's because you've used a lot of magic." The sound of Tracy's voice startles me. I thought she was still by the burning shop. "But how, you've just transitioned?"

Desiree pulls herself up so she can see Tracy, who is standing behind me. "You know I'm a witch?"

"Yes, that was the thing I wanted to talk to you about before you ran away."

I turn around so Desiree doesn't have to use any more energy by lifting her head over my shoulder. Her body relaxes in my hold, and she furrows her brows at Tracy. "So, you've known all this time?"

Tracy doesn't respond, she just nods.

"You should have told me. We're best friends, we tell each other everything...or at least I thought we did."

Deep pink tints Tracy's cheeks. She casts her eyes downward—clearly this is embarrassing and uncomfortable for her. "I'm sorry. Your grandma didn't want to introduce you to this life until you started manifesting powers. There was a great chance you wouldn't inherit the gene, and she wanted to protect you." Then she lifts her eyes to study Desiree. "But, how did you expel so much power? I haven't taught you anything yet."

Desiree bites her bottom lip before answering. "Silla gave me knowledge of my heritage."

"What?" Tracy and I ask in unison.

"I'm a Mortifera."

Did I just here her correctly? She's a Mortifera witch?

192

Tracy swallows loudly. "How do you know that?"

Desiree points to her head. "I told you, she gave me knowledge...when her essence merged with me."

"What?" Tracy's face is one of wonder. "So, you really met with Silla?"

"Yes. That," Desiree points to the once blazing building, "was me. I torched that fiery red-headed monster after he crushed my trachea."

I glance down at Desiree's throat, anger heating the tips of my ears. There is some slight bruising on her throat. I can't believe I didn't see that before now.

"You killed him?" Tracy asks with a smile playing on her lips.

Desiree nods, a yawn forming a large O on her mouth.

"Good." I'm glad that stupid idiot is gone. "Let's get you home, my beautiful girl."

Chapter Forty-Three
Desiree

The warmth and softness of Caleb's comforter is heaven. Rolling over, I snuggle further into its thickness. His scent is everywhere. A smile curves my face. I can't believe I'm in his bed—again. This time around, I plan on staying.

Mittens meows at my shifting, circles around in two complete circles, then paws the comforter before settling in again. I scratch behind her ears. "I missed you." She purrs and rests her warm nose against my hand.

Being kidnapped and held captive by deranged vampires made me realize one thing. In this world, there is good and there is evil. Just because something has the appearance of evil doesn't necessarily mean that it *is* evil.

When Caleb first revealed to me he was a vampire, my thoughts automatically went to blood-sucking murderous monsters with no reflection that burst into flames in the sunlight. Of soulless, undead creatures whose flesh melts at the touch of a crucifix, and are condemned and unable to step foot in a church. At the time, I pictured myself wearing a garlic necklace to repel him.

Now that I've had time to mull this over and experience evil firsthand, I know that Caleb is not evil. He is one of the kindest, gentlest, and most caring people that I know. It's funny how we form opinions based on what we've seen on television or read in a book.

"Good evenin', darlin'." At the sound of Caleb's voice, I roll over. He's standing in the doorway, hip leaning against the frame, holding a plate and a glass of orange juice. "You sleep okay?"

I nod. "What time is it?"

"Just after five." He pushes himself off the doorframe and strides toward the bed.

My eyebrows raise. "What?" I can't believe I slept so long. It was only seven in the morning when we arrived back at his house. "Why did you let me sleep so much?"

He shrugs as if it's no big deal. "You needed it." Siting on the bed, he hands me the glass of orange juice. "You hungry?"

"Yes." Hungry doesn't begin to describe what I am. The last meal I ate was at the diner last night. Add that to whatever the hell my body endured for the transition, plus destroying that psycho vampire, and I'm one hungry witchy woman.

Witchy woman. I try my best not to giggle, but I can't help myself. That term reminds me of a song my grandma used to listen to when I was little. Speaking of her, I need to pay her a visit.

Fork in hand, Caleb cuts a piece of lasagna, blows on it, then puts it to my lips. Its feels odd to have him feed me, but I open my mouth and he guides the fork in. The explosion of flavor when the sauce hits my tongue is out of this world.

Eyes wide, I point to the plate. "Did you make this?"

A smile curves his lips. "Yeah."

"Caleb, this is amazing." He offers me another bite. *Chew. Swallow.* "You should think about opening up a restaurant."

His shoulders shake with laughter. "And who is going to help me run this restaurant so I still have time to oversee the

195

ranch *and* the club?"

I take a sip of the juice. Oh, my goodness, I hadn't realized how thirsty I was. As embarrassing as it is to have him see me gulping the entire glass, I can't stop myself. Casting my eyes down, I place the empty glass on the bedside table, wiping my mouth with the back of my hand.

When I finally push the embarrassment aside, I look up. His gaze is not one of disgust, like I'd been expecting. It's one of concern. "How ya feelin'? Honestly."

"Great." Aside from being hungry and thirsty, I do feel rather amazing. "I feel well-rested; just needing some sustenance, I suppose."

His eyes scan every inch of my face, probably trying to determine whether to believe me. After intently staring into my eyes, he nods. "Good. We'll get you more juice after you've eaten." Scooping up another bite, he puts the fork back to my lips.

Chew. Swallow. "I'm thinking, me."

Fork poised at my lips, unmoving. His brows furrow in confusion. "Huh?"

"Me." I point to myself, as if that makes it all clear.

Tilting his head, he still holds a look of confusion. "You, what?"

Leaning forward, I take the bite that is still suspended in front of my lips. *Chew. Swallow.* "I'll help you run the restaurant."

The look of surprise on his face is priceless. I'm guessing he didn't expect such an answer. Eyes boring into mine, he takes his time studying me. Maybe he's trying to decide whether I'm serious, or whether I could handle the job.

"What? I'm more than capable of overseeing a restaurant part-time. Between the two of us, and with the help of hired management, we can get a restaurant up and running."

His hand is still frozen in mid-air, fork empty from the bite I'd taken previously. Shock is present in his unmoving eyes. What is he thinking? Does he think I'm incompetent? My heart sinks at the possibility of him thinking I'm not smart enough to help him run a business. Oh no, what if he doesn't want me around long-term?

Pushing that last thought aside, I touch his cheek with my fingertips, tracing the line of his jaw. "Talk to me, goose."

Blinking, then blinking again, he continues to stare at me. I'm beginning to second guess what I've said. It's moving too fast, too soon. I open my mouth, ready to retract everything I said about helping him oversee a restaurant, when he finally speaks. "When will you have the time? You spend the majority of your days at the hospital taking care of those sick children."

It isn't incompetency that he fears in me, it's my lack of time. He's right, of course. I am at work more than I am at home. Even so, that doesn't mean I couldn't spend an hour or so in the evenings looking over things, and taking my days off to stop in for a few hours to help in the kitchen.

"Yes, that's true." I cup his face with my hands. "That's what hired management is for. To be there and run things for us. Our job is to oversee. We can each take an hour or two on our busy days to look at numbers and talk to management. Then on our days off we can step in the restaurant for a few hours to do what needs to be done."

There's a pause, and his face transforms into pure happiness. "You're perfect, ya know that?" He drops the fork onto the plate and leans into me, kissing me so tenderly that every fiber of my being comes alive.

His lips are soft and warm, pressing ever so gently. A moan vibrates in the back of my throat. This man, over the course of the short time we've been together, has stolen my heart. I love him like I've never loved another. A love so deep I can't imagine a life without him.

He's my rock, my shelter from the raging storm, the very air that I breathe.

The plate hits the floor, shattering into several pieces and probably splattering lasagna sauce all over the hardwood. With the speed of lightning, he locks the bedroom door and is back on the bed with his shirt off. "You love me."

It's a statement, not a question, but I answer him anyway. "Yes, more than you can imagine."

His nostrils flare when he sucks in a breath. "Say it." As the words leave his mouth, the heat of his breath warms my chin.

He's so close, our lips are just millimeters apart. "I love you." The hazel of his eyes darkens. Is this arousal I see reflecting in his beautiful orbs?

The air hisses as it passes through his teeth. "I've waited my whole life for you." He nips my bottom lip. "You are my moon, my stars, my sun, and my heart."

Butterflies awaken in my belly when his fingertips slip under my shirt, touching the bare skin on my side. Deftly, his fingers trail up my body, brushing against my breast. Goosebumps raise on my flesh; my breathing hitches a notch.

His eyes search mine. "Do you want me?" There's not just arousal in his eyes, there's also promise. Promise of a future, an everlasting love. A promise to protect me for all eternity.

"Yes." My voice is barely a whisper.

"Darlin', once we do this," he glances at the space between our bodies, "we'll be connected in ways you could never imagine in your wildest dreams. We'll be bound, heart and soul, at the uniting of our bodies. Our minds open to each other and our hearts a beacon, drawing us toward one another." Sucking his bottom lip between his teeth, he holds it there while studying my face. "Your body would stop aging, and you'd gain immortality through the union of our bodies."

"Soul mates?" This is like what I've read in my romance novels.

"Yes, darlin'. We're soul mates, and giving ourselves to one another will bind us to the other for eternity."

What he's saying is scary and comforting. Scary for the unknown, but comforting in the fact that we'll be connected in every possible way. I want this, want him. He's mine and I'm his.

Wrapping my arms around his neck, my fingers lace together. "I'm ready." I've never been more ready for anything in my entire life. "Make love to me, Caleb."

Pulling him toward me, I capture his lips. The soft warmth of those luscious lips on mine melt me like butter. Every muscle in my body relaxes and I scoot myself down onto the mattress, bringing him with me.

The muscles in his arm flex as he trails his finger up and down my side, brushing against my breast with each stroke. His tongue caresses the crease of my lips and they part. Taking the invitation, his tongue darts in and immediately tangles with mine, dancing to the beat of a lover's drum.

The butterflies in my belly intensify, creating a wild fire in the depths of my core that spread throughout my body in a rush. He takes his time removing our clothes, kissing every inch of skin that he exposes. "I love you, darlin'."

Running his fingers through my hair, he kisses me gently as he enters me, and we rock to our own rhythm.

Chapter Forty-Four
Caleb

Making love to Desiree was perfect. For the first time in my entire existence, I feel complete. I'm no longer a man just living life, I'm a man who's found the other half of him and is now made whole.

Brushing a lock of hair out of her eyes, I kiss her nose. "You're the prettiest girl in the world."

Heat tints her cheeks a lovely shade of pink. "You're just saying that because I'm lying in your bed naked as the day I was born."

"I'm saying it because," I tap her on the nose with my index finger, "it's true."

Knock. Knock. Knock.

Whoever is knocking on my bedroom door has picked the absolute worst time. "What?" I bark.

"I'm sorry for disturbing you, but I need to speak with you two." Tracy's voice is quiet; she probably knows what's going on behind this door.

Desiree moans and rolls her eyes. "Not now, Trace."

"Des, you know I wouldn't be interrupting mind blowing sex just to have a little chat." She jiggles the doorknob. "Now get dressed and open this door."

Desiree groans. "Tracy...."

Bang. Bang. Bang.

"Caleb," Alex yells. "Ass out of bed. Now."

"All right, now step away from my door before I rip it off the hinges and beat you with it." I groan and roll over, tossing the sheet off my body. Smiling at Desiree, I say, "Looks like we're being summoned." Picking my jeans up off the floor, I slip them on and hand Desiree her clothing.

Once she's fully clothed, I open the door. Tracy is sipping hot tea from a mug, tapping her nails on the ceramic. Alex has his hands on his hips and worry lines on his forehead. What alarms me is the fact that Ursula, Mike, Billy, David, and Joe are standing in formation behind my cousin. All four of my ranch hands have their arms crossed over their chests. So much for a peaceful evening.

I glance over my shoulder at Desiree. That happy afterglow is still burning on her cheeks and neck, but she also senses the tension on the other side of this door. Tracy eases around me and rushes to Desiree's side. Stepping to the side, I wave the others in. They enter, forming a line at the foot of the bed. Alex waits until I'm back at Desiree's side before he says a word. "We just received a call from Mac."

Before he can continue, Desiree interrupts. "It's Drake, isn't it?"

Taking her hand, I twine our fingers together. At first I'm expecting her to be scared, or at the very least nervous. She's not. Not only can I see this in her posture and on her face, but I can feel it in our newly formed bond. My little witchy woman is not at all bothered by the fact that Drake is drawing attention. What she is, is angry that he is hurting innocent people.

Something happened to Desiree while she was being held hostage. Whatever her experience was with Silla, it has changed her. She's stronger, more confident, and definitely houses a lot of power. God almighty, I can feel the power surging through her.

"Yes." Alex continues with his news. "After we rescued you—"

"Correction," Desiree interrupts, raising her finger. "Don't forget who escaped the chains that held me suspended on a lift hook, magically broke through the chain binding the doors that held me captive, *and* killed the vampire that had been sent to keep watch over me."

There's a spark in her that wasn't there before. I love it. Lifting her hand to my lips, I press a kiss to the back of her knuckles.

"Noted," Alex says. "I'm assuming he wasn't happy about your escape and losing one of his men. Mac said that he has left a trail of bodies between that burned down shop and the diner off the highway."

"That's where your scent ended before mixing with Drake's," Ursula states matter-of-factly.

Sorrow fills her eyes as they turn to meet mine. Desiree turns so that we're face to face. "I'm sorry that I ran away from you. I just didn't know how to process the information that was thrown at me."

I cup her face. "I know." There is no need for her to apologize for running away. She was scared, I know that. Her reaction was exactly what I'd expected.

"I didn't want to be followed, so I took a detour through a fruit farm, or whatever it is." She cups my face in her palm, mirroring me. "I regret it, you know?"

I do know. Everything she feels and thinks transmits to me, so I nod.

"Anyway. I was getting cold and tired, so when I found the diner I stopped to get a drink and use the phone. The lovely waitress was kind enough to feed me, free of charge." At the mention of the waitress, her eyes soften. "Oh God, I hope that waitress wasn't harmed."

"Me too, darlin'." If that kind waitress is still alive, I'll have to remember to stop in and personally thank that woman for taking care of the love of my life.

"That's where I met Drake. I had no idea who he was when he came waltzing in. When he started questioning me about my personal life, I tried to walk away but he compelled me. I didn't understand what was happening at the time. It wasn't until my meeting with Silla that I understood what he'd done to me."

Her shoulders slump with thoughts of Drake, and I want nothing more than to wrap her in my embrace and erase those horrid memories.

"And the other vampire working with Drake?" Alex asks.

"I'm not sure how many there were, but the one that I killed had fiery-red hair. The other one that kept watch over me had hair like cotton." Desiree returns her attention to me. "The red-head said he wanted to kill me in front of you. A life for a life." She pauses in thought. "He said something about you sending his mother to Purgatory."

"Charles," Alex and I say in unison.

"Why did Drake target me?" Desiree's question isn't one of trepidation—she's seeking facts about the man that took her hostage.

I trace her jaw with my thumb. "Because he wants to hurt me, to make me pay for locking him and his fledglings away. Drake is as evil as they come. He's tortured countless young women over the centuries. Raping them, slashing their flesh with his teeth, and watching them bleed out. Right before Alex and I captured him and sent him to Purgatory, he'd pulled a young woman's fingers off and forced her to eat them."

Green tints Desiree's face with that knowledge, and I'm

afraid she may spew lasagna all over my bed.

Southern Shade

Chapter Forty-Five
Desiree

Bile is rising in my throat, burning my esophagus. Just hearing about the torture of those poor women makes me sick. A shiver runs down my spine. I can't even imagine the pain they went through. Swallowing the bile down, I shift on the bed, squeezing the corner of the comforter in an attempt to keep my temper at bay. "He's sick. Why is he still allowed to roam the earth? He should be hung for those crimes."

"Oh, I agree with you one-hundred percent." Ursula steps forward and kneels beside the bed. Her eyes lock on mine and she pries the blanket from my hand. "But the problem is, we can't kill an immortal. There is only one weapon out there that is able to kill one of us, and that is a Mortifera."

Nothing can kill a vampire other than whatever the heck I am. Yes, I remember this from my time with Silla. I guess I just expected the vampire council to have the means to execute one of their own. "I don't understand. I mean, I get what you're saying, but how long ago was he locked away?"

Caleb sighs, and the sadness there pulls my attention back to him. "Five hundred years ago...shortly after Charles had my father murdered."

"What?" That's so sad. Just seeing the hurt in his eyes breaks

205

my heart in two. I'm not sure what I'd do if I lost my grandma, especially in a manner such as that. "I'm so sorry, Caleb."

"My father was one of the council leaders." A weak smile graces Caleb's face. "One of the best vampire sergeants I've had the privilege of working under."

"That he was." Alex claps his cousin on the shoulder.

Ice seeps into my veins, freezing everything in its wake. Caleb's father was a vampire and Charles had him murdered? The realization of his words causes my heart to sink to my feet. A vampire is an immortal that cannot be killed by any force other than a Mortifera. I'm a Mortifera. Oh, what he must think of me now that he knows what I am.

Afraid to speak, I stand and make my way to the window. The moonlight shines bright in the night sky. The sounds of the farm animals are faint. They've most likely gone inside their shelters for the evening.

I'm not sure how long I've been standing here staring at the vehicles below, but when Caleb brushes hair off my neck it startles me. "I can hear your thoughts and feel your warring emotions. I know you're wonderin' how I feel about you now that we've discovered what you are."

I can't look him in the eye for fear that I'll see a spark of hatred there. "I'm not sure I could like, let alone love, me if I were in your shoes."

Pinching my chin, he tugs until our eyes meet. "Stop analyzing this. Yes, after my father's murder I hated all witches."

I lower my eyes to the floor.

"Look at me." His command is one that I can't disobey no matter how hard I try. When I look at him I don't see hatred. "The moment Tracy told me that you were a witch I had to make a decision. To continue hating all witches based on one witch's bad behavior, or put my hatred aside and continue loving you."

"But I'm the monster that killed your father."

"No. You're not the monster that killed my father any more than Joe Smoe is a murderer because Jack the Ripper was." His fingers tangle in my hair and his eyes look deep into mine. "The fact that you're a Mortifera does not make you guilty of another's crime. I choose you. Above all else, I choose you."

Tears blur my vision. He chooses me even though I am exactly what he's hated for years. Me. An ordinary girl with zero fashion sense, and a love for all things chocolate. A lump gets stuck in the back of my throat and I have to swallow it down. My heart has never been so full.

"Never doubt my love for you." Tugging gently on my hair, he presses his lips to mine.

"Ahem."

The sound of Tracy ruins my perfect moment. If it weren't for Drake and the amount of destruction he's causing, I would stomp across the room and grab a pillow, then hit her with it. Caleb's hands fall from my hair and he steps to the side, bringing everyone back into my line of view. Tracy shrugs her shoulders as if to say, *sorry.*

"So, why didn't one of the council find a Mortifera to deal with Drake?" As much as I want to avoid Caleb's gaze, I direct my question toward him.

"Mortifera witches are rare." Tracy answers my question as she closes the distance between us. "There is only one family line they are born into." Apparently, my brain is having a hard time connecting the dots, because what she says is not what I'm expecting her to say. When the word leaves her mouth, I gasp. "Rathmoore."

Goosebumps break out on my arms. "Rathmoore is my grandma's ancestral name." I'm not sure why I didn't put the pieces together when she said that Mortifera came from one family line. That would mean that I also come from that line.

"That's right." She takes both of my hands, holding them between us like a lifeline. "Your mother is also a Mortifera. I know that you've believed your whole life that she abandoned you, but that's not true."

My eyes widen. "I don't understand."

"Your mother didn't leave you of her own free will. She was forced to give you up in order to save you from those hunting her."

"Tracy?" Her admission stuns me. I can't even form a complete sentence to ask her what she means.

"Des, your mother was on trial for marrying outside of our race." Tracy squeezes my hands. "We are not supposed to marry and procreate outside of the supernatural race. For your mother, her crime was even greater because of her powerful bloodline. A Mortifera conceiving a child with a human means that there's a high chance the baby will be born without the magical gene."

"Oh." I glance behind me.

Caleb rests his hands on my shoulders, massaging the tension out of my muscles. "Vampires are considered magical. What she means is that the witch council doesn't allow witches to unite with the human race."

Those words are music to my ears. Now that I have Caleb, I could never give him up...not even to save my soul.

Chapter Forty-Six
Caleb

The relief that washes over Desiree's face is a beautiful sight. At this moment, I'm ecstatic that I'm a vampire. I'm not sure I could give her up if I were human. This woman is my whole world. The one person that I want to spend an eternity with.

"Do we know where Drake is?" I ask Ursula.

Ursula shakes her head. "No. Mac doesn't have any more information other than the string of bodies." She crosses her arms over her chest. "And I haven't been out to investigate yet."

"Okay, well, we know who he's after." I pull Desiree against me, wrapping my arms around her. "He hates me, and is willing to kill Desiree to hurt me."

I fully expect her body to tense under my hold, and it surprises me that she stays calm. "Well, I hope he's ready for disappointment." The finality of Desiree's statement leaves no room for doubt. My woman is powerful and more than capable of taking care of this matter. God, I love her.

The sound of spooked horses draws my attention out the window. "You have got to be kiddin' me."

My horses are running amuck and the pigs have been set loose, squealing in fear. Drake is standing outside of my house looking up at the window I'm currently standing in, blood staining his face and shirt. I swear, if he's harmed any of my animals I will break every bone in his body before Desiree can get down there to destroy him.

Rage consumes me and I rush out of the room without so much as an explanation. Thanks to our newly formed bond, Desiree and I are linked. Oh boy, is she mad. Not mad that I'm seeking revenge. Mad that I left her behind to satisfy my itch to break this idiot's bones.

Caleb? Her tone is stern even through telepathy.

It's okay, darlin'.

You heard me? The surprise in her mental voice brings a smile to my face.

Yeah, darlin'. I heard ya. My feet hit the bottom step and I race toward the front door, throwing it wide open. *We're bonded now, remember?*

Oh, right.

"Caleb." Drake takes two large steps in my direction. "Nice to see you're keeping up with your father's farm." Regardless of his statement, his voice is menacing and venom drips from his mouth.

I feel them before they step onto the porch with me.

Ursula steps up to my right side, Alex to my left, and David, Joe, Billy, and Mike are standing behind us.

A cackle leaves Drake and echoes in the night sky. "You think that you're a match for me?" He shakes his head. "Did you think that I'd come to this party unprepared?"

Leaves crunch in the distance. The wind picks up, and leaves and other debris swirl along the ground. I move, my vampire speed getting me to Drake in less than a second. My hand closes around his throat and despite his predicament, a smirk appears on his face.

Before I have time to register why that smirk is in place,

pressure fills my head and causes me to fall to my knees. I can hear Desiree's panicked screams, both telepathically and from her place upstairs at the window. I'd like to reassure her that I'll be fine, but the pain that's constricting my brain like a boa is blocking the signal from my brain to my telepathic voice.

Thunder booms in the sky, rattling every window in my house. Tears well up in my eyes from the pressure in my head. Blinking, the wetness trails down my face and drips to the ground. My eyes widen in horror when I see where my tears have fallen. Red splats of blood stain the grass. *Tears of blood? What in the world is happening to me?*

Drake kneels, gripping my jaw tightly in his hand, forcing my head upright so that our eyes meet. "That's right, pretty boy. I brought my own witch to this shindig." His eyes shine with some form of crazy joy. Releasing me, he stands and cackles at the lot of us on our knees. "Look how pathetic you all are. The bloody tears are only the beginning."

Shiny black hooker-heels come into view; the paint on the woman's toes is a neon pink. It takes every ounce of strength I have to lift my head and look her in the eye. Her jet-black hair is loose, tiny ringlets of curls bouncing with her movements.

The sound of chanting echoes in the night, drawing my attention, and I crane my neck to see around this woman. Behind Drake five women stand, hands linking together, their chants creating lightning in the dark sky. *Just my luck.*

Coughs rack my body. My lungs burn from the onslaught.

The witch standing in front of me points her bony finger at me. "Evomat vermes." A spark ignites and flies from her fingertip and zaps me on the chest.

The coughing increases and my lungs suddenly feel as though they are on fire. Intense pain forces my body forward, and I catch myself with my hands. Thickness rises in my throat and when I cough again, hundreds of worms fly from my mouth. The sight of them make me want to vomit for real.

Drake breaks out into full blown laughter. "Ah, sweet victory." His hiking boot connects with my face.

A loud crack comes from my nose and blood gushes out of my nostrils. That pain, mixing with the worms I'm still coughing up, mixed with the pressure in my head, and I'm left immobile and helpless.

"Now you have an inkling of the pain I've suffered over the last five hundred years. Just an inkling. Purgatory is no playground. Maggots eat your flesh daily, and fire burns the skin from your bones with no hope of relief." Drake's boot swings back and rushes toward my face, this time connecting with my throat.

The pressure on my throat causes me to choke on the worms. Their squirmy bodies wiggle, which makes me gag. Toppling over onto my side, I have a clear view of my house. All my comrades are on their knees, gripping their heads, likely from the pain the witches are causing them. Then my beacon of hope fills the doorway.

Desiree.

Chapter Forty-Seven
Desiree

Drake has brought witches to this fight. I stare down at Caleb, who is lying on the ground in pain and retching. At the sight of Drake kicking Caleb, not once but twice, I'm beyond angry. Rage boils within my veins. That monster is about to find out just who he is up against.

I turn to storm out of the room and a hand catches hold of my wrist, tugging until I come to a stop. I look up at Tracy, concern in her eyes. "Des, you can't go down there and stand against all of those witches on your own. You may be a Mortifera, but that doesn't mean that his little coven won't overpower you."

The love of my life is in danger, and hell would have to freeze over before I'd stay up here and allow those lowlifes to continue their torture. "Look, if I end up dead trying to protect him, then so be it. I refuse to stand by and watch them hurt the man that I love." I let out a breath. "Trace, I love him more than life itself."

"I get it." Tracy's eyes are soft, pleading with me to listen to what she needs to say. "But alone, you're no match for their power. I can feel their strength through these walls."

I nod, I can feel it too.

"Channel me."

I raise a brow. "What?"

She takes my other hand in hers so that we form our own tiny circle. "Close your eyes and focus on my power, pull it into yourself, and allow it to merge with yours."

I have no idea what she's talking about. Channel her? Okay, I don't know what the heck I'm doing, but I'll give it a shot. Closing my eyes, I focus on her, on her witchy power residing within her. It's strong—my best friend is one heck of a powerful witch.

Her power reaches out to me like tendrils, seeking a connection. I focus on those tiny snake-like stems, my soul beckoning them with open arms. Those tendrils slither toward my inner being, wrapping around and merging with my power.

Warmth spreads through my veins, sparks igniting at my fingertips. Her power fuels my own, and my body hums with the added energy. I feel invincible. *I wonder if this is what the Hulk feels like when he transforms?*

I open my eyes. Surprise fills me when I find a bright white glow radiating from my pores. Releasing Tracy's hands, I watch as she opens her eyes. They widen when she takes in my glowing appearance. "Desiree?"

The look of awe on her face stuns me. "What?"

Opening her mouth, she starts to speak but clamps her lips shut instead. After a moment, she gives her head a slight shake. "I've never seen anything like this."

"What?" I glance down at myself. "What do you mean?"

Tracy points at the glow surrounding my body. "This. I've seen channeling, participated in channeling. But this, this is something else altogether."

Did I do something wrong? Her words echo in my head, setting my nerves on edge. "I don't understand. I did what you asked me to."

"And you did great." Tracy taps my nose. "You're a powerful witch. I've never seen anything like that."

"So, I didn't do anything wrong?"

She shakes her head, a smile on her face. "No, you did everything right." Reaching out, she takes my hand. "You are the most powerful witch I've ever seen, and I've seen a lot."

Laughter makes its way through the glass. I peer out the window and see Drake—his back arches, and he's cackling like a crazed maniac. The sight of him enjoying Caleb's torment fuels my anger. Lightning lights up the sky in response to my emotions, and the witches look up at the bolts with confusion, and maybe a hint of fear.

I turn and march from the room, down the stairs, and throw the front door open with enough force I know it leaves a dent in the sheetrock. As I step onto the porch, Tracy at my side, I lift my hands toward the sky.

Lightning crackles and thunder booms. With a flick of my finger, the bolts race downward, striking the coven of witches that stand a few yards away and setting their bodies on fire. Drake hisses in anger and darts forward, his hand stretching out toward me.

I lift my hand and mentally inflict crushing pain at Drake. This causes him to fall to his knees, a howl escaping his lips. The witch at his side steps forward, arm stretching toward me. "Non aer."

At her words, my throat tightens and air ceases to flow into my lungs. Tracy links her hand with mine to ramp up my power, but I can't concentrate on anything aside from my burning lungs. The witch steps closer and the moonlight hits her face, giving me the perfect view. My eyes widen in shock. I know this woman. Not personally; I've only ever seen pictures of her at home. Grandma had pictures of her lining the walls in the hallway. Tracy gasps and my eyes seek hers.

This witch of Drake's stretches out her other hand toward

215

Tracy. "Non aer."

Tracy's grip on my hand loosens, her other hand clawing at the collar of her shirt as she seeks oxygen. Seems both of us are suffering from our airways being closed from a magical force.

Aunt Deidra, I mouth.

Her eyes widen when she reads my lips, but her magical grip on my airway doesn't budge. "Desiree?"

I nod.

Her glare turns toward Drake. "You brought me here to kill my own blood?"

Drake's eyes dart between the two of us, hardening at the realization of who we both are. "Listen to me, Deidra, you will do as I say. We have a blood covenant."

Her head drops and she lets out a long sigh. "I'm sorry, Desiree. I made a blood covenant with him. If I break it then the magic that sealed our agreement will consume me in fire."

A tear escapes her eye and she moves forward. Tracy falls to her knees, her face beginning to turn blue. The amped up magic in my blood provides me with enough oxygen to prevent me from experiencing cyanosis.

A bolt of lightning zig zags through the sky, striking the ground an inch from Deidra's foot. In her shock, her magical hold slips enough for me to take in a gulp of air.

Drake falls to his knees, screaming in agony. At first, I wonder if my aunt has come to her senses and is attacking Drake, but her focus is solely on me. So, who is helping me by attacking my enemy?

A shadow to my right moves in our direction, and my eyes fly to the intruder. A tall, slender woman steps out from the shadows and lifts her hands toward Deidra. Deidra stumbles from the magical blow and falls on her backside.

Beside me, Tracy gasps, sucking in air. I offer her a hand and help her to her feet. We link our fingers together and face the newest threat, ready to attack if need be. The woman continues in our direction, and when the moonlight shines on her face, I get weak in the knees. My emotions are now a rollercoaster, and I'm lost for words.

"Hi, baby girl." She reaches forward and tucks a stray hair behind my ear. "There's not been a day that's gone by that I haven't thought about you."

"Mom?"

"Yes, sweetheart." Her black hair blows in the breeze, and her brown eyes blink back the tears pooled in her dark orbs.

Deidra stands on shaky legs with regret in her eyes. "I'm sorry, Amelia." She lifts both hands and wind swirls around, creating a mini tornado. "I've entered into a blood covenant. You know I can't take it back. I wish I could."

My mother flicks a finger at her sister and Deidra grips her own neck like she's struggling for air.

I smirk at my aunt. "Not so fun, is it?"

My mother then locks her hand with mine. "Together, we'll defeat our enemy."

Warmth seeps into my palms where we're connected, her magic entering my body and merging with mine, adding strength to my already amped up power. Together, we lift our hands toward our enemy. Drake's eyes bulge when he sees the power radiating around us.

I hold Drake's stare. "Mortem."

Bright white flame ignites his body. Agonizing screams tear from his throat and echo through the night. The flame twirls in a tornado-like fashion, then bursts, sending ash up to blow in the breeze.

My mom looks down at her sister. After a minute, she looks at me, then at Tracy. "Tracy, link hands with Desiree and chant with me." We nod, no questions asked. "Ad conteram sigillum." We chant those three words with my mom, over and over.

Chapter Forty-Eight
Caleb

The stabbing pain in my head is finally subsiding. I stand on wobbly legs, offering a hand to Alex. Glancing back at Desiree, I see her holding hands with Tracy and the newcomer. Had I heard right, is this Desiree's momma? I can sense the others pushing themselves up from the ground. Alex is at my side. He doesn't say a word, just watches as Desiree, her momma, and Tracy chant, directing their powers at the woman Desiree had called Aunt Deidra.

"Ad conteram sigillum," the three of them chant steadily in unison.

"I can't believe what I'm seeing." Ursula steps up to my right side. "They're unbinding Deidra's blood covenant."

"What?" Alex and I ask at the same time. Unbinding a blood covenant? Is that even possible?

"They are unweaving the magic binding Deidra to her covenant with Drake." With fascination in her eyes, Ursula continues watching the sight unfolding before us. "I've never seen any witch do such a thing."

Black and white flames swirl around Deidra, tangling and warring with each other. I imagine the black flames represent evil and the white represent good. Shaking uncontrollably, Deidra falls to the ground on her hands and knees. Pain mars her face. Her mouth is a tight line and tears run freely down her cheeks, dripping onto the dead grass.

The flames continue to poke and twist together, creating a wall, blocking my view of the witch. A scream erupts from Deidra's throat and the flames swell, then burst, raining fire that snuffs out before hitting the dead grass. Deidra stands, gasping for breath, and I rush to stand behind Desiree. I have no idea if her covenant has been broken, but I'll be damned if I let her lay a hand on Desiree without a fight. Deidra holds her hands up in surrender, and the three witches relax their stances.

Desiree pulls her hand from her momma's grip, then Tracy's. Turning around, she smiles up at me, jumping into my arms and planting a kiss on my lips. I hold her tight against my body, not willing to let her go. Her legs wrap around my waist, locking us together. "I was so afraid I wouldn't get to you in time," she speaks against my lips.

Kissing her nose, I smile. "You did great, darlin'."

The sound of Tracy clearing her throat pulls my attention away from Desiree. "You lovebirds need to get a room."

Pink tints Desiree's neck and cheeks. This look is adorable on her. In her embarrassment, she rests her forehead against mine before unwinding her legs from around my waist. I don't want to lose this contact — she feels so good against my body — but we still have other matters to contend with, so I reluctantly put her back on her feet.

Turning in my arms, Desiree rests her head back on my chest as we watch her momma close the distance between her and Deidra. "Deidra, how could you enter into a covenant with a lunatic like that?"

Wiping tears from her face, Deidra glances our way wearing a sad expression, then locks eyes with Amelia. "I'm sorry, sister.

I had no other choice."

"We always have a choice." Amelia crosses her arms over her chest, back ramrod straight and toe tapping the ground. "You know you're not the first to ever be approached for such a task. Some of us have had the decency to decline." She sighs, full of exasperation. "You're a Mortifera, for God's sake. You have a responsibility to serve and protect."

Deidra's head hangs in shame. "Drake needed a Mortifera to destroy a vampire, and he threatened to kill my son if I didn't comply. He said he had one of his men trailing Matt at the university in Oregon. My boy is young and has not yet transformed. I didn't know that Desiree was involved. I swear." Sobs rack the woman's body, and I immediately feel sorry for her.

I can't imagine being in Deidra's position. Having a target on your kid and being forced to do things against your will. I'm glad that Drake is dead and can no longer go around tormenting innocent people. I know I'll be sleeping peacefully now that's he's been dealt with.

Amelia gasps at her sister's words, uncrossing her arms. "He threatened Matt?"

Deidra nods, pleading with her eyes for Amelia to believe her.

Amelia steps forward, gazing down at her sister. "I do believe you, Deidra. It's been too long since we last saw one another." Desiree's momma wraps her arms around her sister, and the two of them weep.

At the sight of the two women bonding, Mike, Billy, David, and Joe quietly make their way down the porch steps and rush to round up the loose animals.

Taking her cue, Ursula rests her hand on my shoulder. "Looks like my work here is done, even if I didn't do much." Thrusting her hand out to Desiree, she says, "It was nice meeting you."

"It was nice meeting you too." Desiree takes the hand Ursula offers and the two of them smile.

"Caleb, I'll see you around." Ursula gives me a wave before heading to her rental car.

Exhaustion fills my bones and I cannot wait to get inside, relax, and drink a glass or two of blood. My body hurts, and my energy level is way too low for my liking.

Heavy breathing comes from Alex as he steps in front of us, blocking my view of Desiree's family. "So, what…we're just going to let that woman," he jerks his thumb behind him, "get away with attempted murder?" The rage in his eyes is murderous.

Desiree stiffens in my arms. No doubt those words sting her heart. This is a family that she never had the chance to get to know. "That *woman* is Desiree's family," I state sternly. Jeez, my cousin can be a jerk sometimes.

His eyes narrow. "And she damn near killed all of us." His shout echoes in the night. Anger rolls off Alex in waves. Glancing down at Desiree, then at the women behind him, and finally at me, he lets out a huff. Stomping like an errant child, he walks around us and enters the house. "You better pray this doesn't end badly," he calls over his shoulder.

I know it took a lot for my cousin to walk away without killing Desiree's aunt. As a soldier, it's in his nature to make sure all guilty parties are dealt with, but this situation is different. Desiree's aunt didn't set out to purposely harm any of us. She was threatened, and because of my love for Desiree I can understand why she went along with that lunatic. If anyone were to threaten Desiree's life, I'd do whatever it took to ensure her safety.

The two women make their way up the porch steps. Deidra's eyes are cast to the ground, and her shoulders slump. This woman is clearly ashamed of her actions. If she were anyone else, I'd order her to leave and never come near my city again. Since she's Desiree's aunt, I'll let my soul mate decide what she wants, and I'll stand behind that decision one hundred percent, regardless of my feelings.

Dropping her arms from her sister, Desiree's momma extends her hand out to me. "Hello. I'm Desiree's mother, my name is Amelia." I shake her hand. The smile on her face reminds me of Desiree's. My little witchy woman is a spittin' image of her momma. Looking between the two of us, she says, "It's so good to see that Desiree has found a good man to love her."

My arm tightens around Desiree's waist. "I'd give my life for her."

"I can see that." Placing her hand on Deidra's back, Amelia shoves her sister forward. "This is my sister, Deidra. I know we have a lot to talk about where she is concerned." She glances at her sister, worry lines forming on her face. "I don't want to see her persecuted for being forced into a blood covenant with a psychopath. Surely you can understand doing whatever necessary for those you love?"

I must admit, I would have done the same thing had Drake threatened Desiree, but that still doesn't ease my anger. The witch would have killed me without a second thought, would have killed her own niece had Amelia not shown up. "I understand that, but she was willing to trade the life of one family member for another. That's unforgivable in my book." I place a kiss to the top of Desiree's head. "But I'll stand by whatever decision Desiree makes."

The sound of a chair crashing into the wall sounds from inside the house, and immediately following are a few expletives from Alex. There's no way he will forgive and forget. Ever.

Waving my hand toward the open door, I say, "Come on in. I'll brew a pot of coffee and we can chat."

223

Chapter Forty-Nine
Desiree

Alex keeps his mouth shut while my mom and aunt are in the house. I know this is hard for him to hear. To him, my aunt is nothing more than another killer. I agree. Her actions are unforgiveable, but she is also my family. I can't just give up all hope for the woman that shares my blood. Surely he can see that.

A pot of coffee and a plate of leftover lasagna later, and our little visit is coming to an end. My aunt has apologized profusely for her behavior, and I'm choosing to give her the benefit of the doubt and forgive her. Though I will never turn my back to her. I'll be keeping an eye on that woman for as long as I live.

Aunt Deidra shakes my hand. "I'm really sorry for tonight." She looks toward the kitchen, where Alex is still pacing. "I think its best that I leave and head back to Washington. Now that we know the threat to Matt is gone, I can sleep easy."

While Aunt Deidra was explaining her situation, my mom made a call to a vampire friend of hers and he apprehended Drake's minion. The minion who was posing as a classmate and friend of Matt's. The very one living in Matt's dorm, and waiting for his cue to rip my cousin's throat out.

Opening the front door, Aunt Deidra turns to me. "I'm thinking of planning a trip back here to visit Mom. I'd like to bring Matt with me. He's never met his grandma." Her eyes dart back and forth between mine and my mother's. "That is, if it's okay with the two of you?"

Personally, I can't wait to meet my cousin—he's just two years younger than me, and is in medical school. Looks like we have a lot in common. "I think that would be great. Grandma would love to see you guys."

"Good." Aunt Deidra steps over the threshold, then turns and waves.

"I'm afraid I must be going. I don't want the witch council tracking me here." My mom reaches out and takes my hands in hers. "You are so beautiful, Desiree. I love you more than you know."

Caleb's arms wrap around my waist. "Amelia, you and Morgan can come back. Desiree needs her parents—she's missed so much." My mom opens her mouth, but Caleb speaks before she can utter a word. "I wouldn't mind turning him into a vampire. The council can't do anything if he's one of us."

The smile that spreads on my mom's face is priceless. "I'll let him know." She looks back at me. "He misses you too." This makes me happy. "I'll call as soon as he's made a decision." Giving me a kiss on the cheek, my mom walks out of the house.

After watching my mom leave, I shut the door and turn into Caleb's arms. The night's events have worn me out, and tears are falling from my eyes due to my rollercoaster of emotions. Caleb allows me to cry on his shoulder, his hand rubbing gentle circles on my back.

The sound of my cell phone ringing cuts through the silence. Alex races to the library where I left it, bringing it back to me in lightning speed. "Thanks." He nods. "Hello?"

"Desiree?" Nurse Johnson's voice startles me. Why would she be calling?

"Yes?"

"I'm calling because you're the nurse in charge of Elijah Goodman." My heart sinks when she says his name. He was in such bad health when I saw him yesterday. "His parents were in a horrible accident." She pauses and my heart drops. "They didn't make it."

I suck in a breath of air and clear my throat. "Does he have any living relatives?"

Her response is immediate. "None."

Caleb cups my face, kissing my nose. "We'll adopt him." I furrow my brows, but then remember he has super hearing. He knows how I feel about this boy because my emotions are exploding out to him, revealing my desires. I want to be a mom to Elijah.

I smile at the man I love more than anyone in the world. "Jamie, make the call, but you be sure to let them know I plan on adopting that little man."

Her smile emits through her voice. "Done."

Alex steps into the room just as I shut off my cell phone and place it in my back pocket. "Mac." He stops talking and looks between us, most likely reading Caleb's mind. He now knows about Elijah. Shaking his head, he continues. "He is at one of the crime scenes now, a car crash. A man and woman. There is a diaper bag and a car seat with them, but no baby. The official report will state that a bear broke into their vehicle and attacked them, but the truth is, Drake ripped their bodies apart and carved the Xavier symbol into their foreheads. They were dead when the paramedics arrived. I'm going to assume they are the parents of the boy you've decided to adopt."

"I'm glad he's dead." The words leave my mouth before I think better of it. But honestly, I'm not one bit sorry I said it. Drake was a monster and deserved what he got.

Epilogue
Desiree

It's been three weeks since that horrible night, and now that the threat is gone, I've moved in with Caleb. It's been an adjustment, but it's a good adjustment. It didn't take much persuasion for him to agree to open that restaurant, and I'm excited for a change in jobs. I've resigned at the hospital. Instead of working twelve hours four days a week, I will be volunteering a couple of hours a week. This allows me the time needed to get the restaurant up and running, and will allow me time to be home with Elijah.

Speaking of Elijah, Caleb met with his doctor friend at the hospital and made arrangements for the doctor to inject Elijah with some of Caleb's blood. Caleb's blood has corrected all the damage with our baby's body, and now our boy is happy and healthy.

"What's goin' on in that pretty head of yours?" Caleb threads his fingers with mine.

"Just thinking about the past few weeks." I turn in his arms, planting a kiss on his lips. "Thank you."

His brow raises. "What are ya thankin' me for, darlin'?"

"For being an amazing man." Leaning into his embrace, I rest my head in the crook of his neck. "You make me so happy."

"And you have made me the happiest man alive." It's now

227

that I notice he has one hand behind his back, and I'm curious what he's hiding from me.

I tug on his arm but it doesn't budge. "What are you hiding?"

"I'm not hiding anything." He takes a step back.

"Not hiding anything, my foot. You're a little liar."

He smiles, gets down on one knee, and reveals the tiny black box he had hidden behind his back. My hand covers my mouth when I realize what he's holding. Opening the box, he looks up at me and says, "Desiree, my beautiful girl, would ya do me the honor of marryin' me?"

I lower myself to the floor and wrap my arms around his neck, kissing his cheek, his nose, his forehead, and then his mouth. "Yes."

He slides the ring on my finger and kisses me, caressing my tongue with his. Our moment is blissful and my heart is so full. I have a soon-to-be husband and a son. My life is amazing.

His cell phone rings and he stands, pulling me up with him. Plucking the device out of his back pocket, he slides his finger over the screen to answer the call. "Hello?" A smile brightens his face as he listens to the person on the other side of that call. "Yes, we're ready to bring our boy home."

An ear-splitting grin quickly spreads on my face at the mention of our son. Yes, our son. Thoughts of Elijah's happy face fill my mind. I'm so lucky to have the privilege of being his mother.

The adoption process didn't take long to complete, thanks to one of Caleb's vampire friends who owns his own law firm. We were officially his parents two days after that mess with Drake.

It takes me five seconds to grab my purse and start toward the front door. Caleb is close on my heels. As we approach the truck, he opens the passenger door and lifts me into the massive truck before claiming his spot behind the wheel.

"You know, we'll have to get a minivan or some other family vehicle, right?"

He turns the key in the ignition and smiles. "Anything for you and our boy."

Driving to the hospital seems to take forever, and I bounce my leg the entire way. Once the hospital comes into view, I clap my hands and shimmy in my seat. Caleb chuckles at me, but I can't help my excitement.

The truck pulls into the parking garage of the hospital. Rounding the truck, Caleb helps me down and threads our fingers together. "Ready to go get our son?"

I beam up at him. "Yes. I've been ready."

When the elevator doors open to the second floor, we find Tracy waiting for us at the nurse's station with blue balloons in hand. She jumps up and down like a school girl. "I can't wait to spoil my nephew. He'll have all the noisy toys I can find."

I laugh at my friend's enthusiastic excitement.

"Not if I buy them first." I crane my neck to see around Tracy. Alex is standing on the other side of the counter, crossing his arms, and has a smirk on his face. "Make no mistake, Tracy, I plan to give my nephew everything he could ever want...and then some."

I laugh at these two, shaking my head. They're fighting over who will be buying what for my son. I walk past them and enter room 212. Elijah is in the arms of one of the nurses, cooing. When she sees me, she stands and places him in my arms.

Elijah smiles wide when his eyes meet mine. I kiss the tip of his nose. "Come on, baby boy. Let's go home."

About the Author

Tich is an Oklahoma resident and the mother of five. Her passion for reading started at an early age when her Aunt Vicky gave her the novel Heidi for Christmas. She didn't start writing until middle school, after being inspired by her best friend's short stories. "Genny's stories weren't just great but they inspired me to put my pen and paper to good use."

About the Author

Shalisha is an Oklahoma resident, an avid reader, and an author. She has three beautiful daughters and three wonderful grandsons, one of which has Prader-Willi syndrome. Spending time with her family and reading are her favorite pastime. In addition to writing, she is an advanced Med Aide.

About the Author

www.ingramcontent.com/pod-product-compliance
Lightning Source LLC
Chambersburg PA
CBHW021247170626
46807CB00010BA/562